Praise for *Super Schnoz and the Gates of Smell*

★ "The writing, stylistically, has enough action and danger to keep it on the right side of parody, as well as a sense of humor that deftly mixes the absurd with gross-out jokes and clever wordplay. Super Schnoz smells like a winner, especially for reluctant readers."—*Kirkus Reviews*

"With a superhero story line, short chapters, and gross-out humor, the book hits a number of reluctant-reader marks... The book is wacky from page one."—*School Library Journal*

"The puns, references, and nose jokes abound, but themes of friendship and determination are also explored."—*Library Media Connection*

Praise for *Super Schnoz and the Invasion of the Snore Snatchers*

"Bountiful in his nose-related wordplay, Urey crafts fast-moving chapters full of gross-out humor that will surely appeal to reluctant readers and connoisseurs of middle school jokes." —*School Library Journal*

SUPER SCHNOZ

and the Gates of Smell

GARY UREY

pictures by ethan long

ALBERT WHITMAN & COMPANY
CHICAGO, ILLINOIS

To Melissa, Tiana, and Sophie—**G.U.**

For Patrick Byrne—**E.L.**

Library of Congress Cataloging-in-Publication Data

Urey, Gary.
Super Schnoz and the Gates of Smell / Gary Urey ; pictures by Ethan Long.
pages cm
Summary: An eleven-year-old boy with a massive nose becomes an unlikely superhero
when a criminal organization plots to destroy his school.
[1. Nose—Fiction. 2. Smell—Fiction. 3. Superheroes—Fiction. 4. Schools—Fiction.
5. Humorous stories.] I. Long, Ethan, illustrator. II. Title. III. Title: Gates of Smell.
PZ7.U67Su 2013
[Fic]—dc23
2013011511

Printed in the United States of America
10 9 8 7 6 5 4 3 2 1 LB 20 19 18 17 16 15

Cover design by Ellen Kokontis

For information about Albert Whitman & Company,
visit our web site at www.albertwhitman.com.

CHAPTER 1

JUST LIKE A DOG

My name is Andy Whiffler and I was born with a humongous honker.

I'm talking a nose so big it should have come with a warning label, a schnoz so enormous little people could use it as a sledding hill, a pie sniffer so massive that if someone was walking beside me and I turned my head suddenly to the left, I'd knock them out cold.

You get the idea.

The weird thing is that everyone else in my family has adorable little button noses. Noses so perfect they'd make a supermodel jealous.

There's a reason why I have a huge beak. When my

mom was pregnant with me, the pharmacist mixed up her pre-natal vitamins with a steroid for nasal congestion. The effect was disastrous. The steroid overstimulated a gland in my brain that made my nose grow and keep on growing. And I can never have a nose job because there's a major artery that connects from my nasal septum to my brain.

If I snip off my snout, I'm a goner.

Besides the lawsuit money, there's only one good thing that came from the ordeal—I have an amazing sense of smell. I'm talking super-power worthy. I was around the age of two when I first became aware of this talent. My earliest memory is sitting in the living room when a luscious aroma wafted into my nostrils.

Chocolate-chip cookies.

My nose told me the smell wasn't coming from our kitchen. I toddled out the door in my diaper and walked into the street. Since Mom was asleep on the couch and Dad was at work, no one saw me leave.

The sweet scent led me across a main highway, through an auto salvage yard, across a set of busy railroad tracks, and finally to a little white house with yellow curtains. The two-mile journey took me four hours to complete.

The screen door was open and I walked inside. There, sitting on the kitchen table, were several dozen freshly baked cookies. When the old lady who lived there found me, cheeks smeared with chocolate and half her cookies gone, she nearly had a heart attack.

But not as bad as the heart attack my mom almost had when she woke up and discovered me missing. An Amber Alert quickly went out. The cops found me at the old lady's house and delivered me back home.

But that didn't stop me.

Over the next few weeks, when Mom wasn't looking, I escaped from our house and headed straight for the house of cookies. Finally, Mom took me to see a doctor.

After an MRI, they discovered that my olfactory bulbs had quadrupled in size. That means that my sense of smell is a hundred thousand times more powerful than any human.

Just like a dog.

CHAPTER 2

SCHNOZBERRY

A week after I turned eleven my parents bought a house in Denmark, New Hampshire, which meant a new school. My first day at James F. Durante Elementary, kids stared at the mass of fleshy cartilage in the center of my face.

"Can I touch it?" a girl wearing a purple dress asked.

A boy with two missing front teeth gently stroked the bridge of my nose. "Is it real? Or is it made of rubber, like on a Halloween mask?"

"It's real," I answered. "I was born…"

Before I could get out another word, Jimmy Winkler, ape-sized hulk of fifth grade, flicked my right nostril hard with his fingertip. The kid was so big my nose only came up to his chest.

"Ouch!" I yelped. "That hurt!"

"Hey, Honker Face!" Jimmy howled.

His two friends, TJ and Mumps, joined in the fun. TJ was tall and skinny with big teeth and braces. He wore a gray sweatshirt that read: *Will Fight Scary Monsters for Food.* Mumps, on the other hand, looked like a miniature marine with his football jersey, camouflage cargo pants, and crew cut.

"No, he's more like Elephant Face!" TJ said.

"Andy the Big-Nosed Reindeer!" chimed Mumps.

"Pickle Sniffles!" Jimmy screeched. "The Vacuum!" All three of them fell on the hallway floor, laughing like wild hyenas.

Over the next few weeks, Jimmy, Mumps, and TJ called me every name in the book. I was Pinocchio one day, Booger Beak the next. Finally, all the nicknames gave way to just one.

Schnoz—short for Schnozberry.

It's from a line in that old *Willy Wonka and the Chocolate Factory* movie. The scene when everyone is licking the wall paper. On the day before Thanksgiving break, every kid in class was excited about Turkey Day and couldn't focus on schoolwork. So our teacher, Mrs. Field, put on the *Willy Wonka* DVD for the afternoon. She left the room to make copies, but nobody goofed off because we were so into the movie. When Willy shouted "The schnozberries taste like schnozberries!" I made the mistake of asking the question, "What are schnozberries?"

The class roared with laughter.

Jimmy jumped out of his seat, towering over me. "They're boogers, Booger Boy! Nostril turds, snot-rockets, slimy junk dripping from your face trunk!"

"You have the biggest schnoz ever," TJ said. "You should know all about schnozberries."

Mumps raised his fist in the air, shouting, "Schnozberry! Schnozberry! Schnozberry!"

The rest of the class joined in the chant. I wanted to jump out of my seat and run home. As the mantra grew louder, I looked around the room. One girl, Vivian Ramirez, wasn't saying a word. She just sat there quietly with her shaggy black hair, staring right at me.

CHAPTER 3

THE WONDERFUL WORLD OF AROMAS

Most of the kids I know like collecting things. At my last school, a guy named Tyler had over three hundred of his boogers smeared inside a scrapbook. A third-grade girl got her picture in the school newsletter because she saved apes. Not for real, she just clipped pictures of gorillas from nature magazines and taped them on her bedroom wall. A middle schooler from my old neighborhood melted plastic army men in the microwave then molded them into mutant space avengers. He had over sixty-seven sculptures lining his trophy shelf.

As for me, I collect smells.

It doesn't matter if they're stinky, sweet, bitter, rancid, or savory—I love them all! Inside my brain is a detailed catalog of over 967 smells. I add more every day. It's like a scent dictionary, everything from foot fungus to fallen leaves, earwax to ears of corn, road kill to raspberries, morning breath to marshmallows.

So when Mrs. Field assigned us to do a five-minute oral report in front of the class on any topic, naturally, I picked the wonderful world of aromas.

When the day came, I was totally ready. Mrs. Field called kids in alphabetical order. Since my last name begins with *W*, I was at the end— right after Vivian Ramirez's presentation on the twisted-wing parasite, Rory Simon's poem about his new collie puppy, and TJ Tedesco's PowerPoint of his summer vacation to Mount Rushmore.

"The sculptures are huge," TJ said. "In fact, Schnoz's nose and the one carved on Abraham Lincoln's face are about the same size!"

The whole class laughed out loud. I slowly sunk into my seat. If my beak weren't so big, I

would have slid under my desk and hid for the rest of the day.

"Speaking of Andy," Mrs. Field said. "What is your topic?"

"Smells," I said.

The class cracked up again, this time louder than before.

The teacher shot a stern glare that quieted everyone down. "Interesting," she said. "We're ready when you are."

I took a deep breath, tilted my head back, and pointed at the two colossal caverns that were my nostrils. "Everything starts here," I said. "Right up your nose."

"Schnoz's nose holes are so big I could drive my bike through them." I heard Jimmy's voice whisper.

"Gross," said TJ. "You'd probably drown in all the snot."

"Our nose is not only built to smell," I continued, "but to moisten the air we breathe." I plucked out a nose hair and held it up for the class. It was over three inches long. "The hairs in our nostrils filter dust and pollen and junk. Last summer, a barn swallow flew up my nose. It was trying to build a nest. The bird got trapped by my hairs and I was able to pick it out."

"And everyone thought my twisted-wing parasite was disgusting," Vivian muttered. "A living bird up your nose is way nastier."

I ignored her comment, reached into my backpack, and pulled out ten small vitamin bottles.

"Inside each bottle is a different smell," I said. "Remember in art class last week when we worked on collages using different materials? Well, I have made a smell collage."

Mrs. Field's face twisted into question mark. "What may I ask are in those bottles?"

"Scents representing a whole palette of aromas," I said. "It works like this." I dipped each of my ten fingers inside a different bottle and fanned them in front of my face. "On my left hand are the following odors: dirty socks, dog saliva, strawberry Pop Tart, rotting mussel shells, and bacon drippings. On my right hand is toenail fungus, black licorice, boiled cabbage…"

Mrs. Field's face turned three shades of green. Two girls in the front row started gagging and the other kids covered their noses. Jimmy, Mumps, and TJ were in the back row sniggering.

My nostrils deflated.

I couldn't even share my love of smells without people laughing at me.

CHAPTER 4

G AND T

Y ou've heard the old saying: big nose equals big brain.

It's true. I'm wicked smart. The teachers at my old school hated to see me move. I pretty much single-handedly skyrocketed the class average on every standardized test we took. My fourth grade teacher, Mr. Horn, won the Massachusetts teacher of the year—all because of me.

So I wasn't surprised when Mrs. Field recommended me for the Gifted and Talented program in math and reading.

The kids in G and T got to leave the classroom every day for an hour after lunch for specialized, advanced instruction.

"Andy, Sam, Vivian, Nicole, Julia," Mrs. Field announced, "you may walk quietly to Ms. Thurston's room."

As we filed out the door, Mrs. Field stopped us. "Oops," she said. "Wait, children, I forgot another student. TJ Tedesco, you're excused as well."

I couldn't believe my ears! Did she really say TJ Tedesco? One of Jimmy's hairy-knuckled goons was actually in G and T. With his crew cut and camouflage pants, the kid looked like he'd just gotten out of juvenile detention. I watched nervously as TJ got up, slapped his friends a high-five, and then joined us in the hall.

"Ever hear of a moa?" TJ asked me.

I shook my head, my nostrils flapping like elephant ears.

"It's a huge flightless bird that used to live in New Zealand. It's supposed to be extinct, but I have a theory. Maybe it hasn't disappeared at all. It's alive and well and living up your schnozzle!"

TJ reached out to tweak my nose. I ducked and he accidently grabbed Vivian by the hair.

"Knock it off!" Vivian yelled.

Principal Cyrano rounded the corner. "Lower your voice, Vivian," he said. "You know the rules—quiet in the halls."

Vivian's lips pursed; her light brown face turned raspberry red. "Sorry," she mumbled and kept walking.

Ms. Thurston's room was right off the library. There were four long tables, shelves of books, computer stations, and a big window looking out onto the teachers' parking lot.

"Welcome to Gifted and Talented, everyone," Ms. Thurston said. She had short brown hair, a tiny nose, and bright green eyes.

"Hello, Ms. Thurston," everyone said in unison.

"You must be Andy, our new student." Ms. Thurston held out her hand.

"Nice to meet you," I said, shaking her hand. "What do you want me to do?"

"You're going to join TJ and Vivian for a math worksheet. Let me get the other kids started with their reading assignments."

I sat down next to TJ and Vivian and opened

my notebook. I tensed up my nostrils in case TJ tried to grab my nose again.

Vivian rolled up the sleeves of her black sweater and whispered to me, "It's hard to believe, but after me, and now maybe you, TJ's the smartest kid in school. He's a whiz with computers." She turned away and started working on her math problem.

"You must really love black," I said, trying to continue the conversation. "It's the only color you ever wear."

"For your information, black isn't a color. It's a way of life." Vivian opened a black notebook, ripped out a page to use as scratch paper, and completely ignored me. The math worksheet Ms. Thurston gave us was on proportional ratios. The questions were hard, but I breezed through the problems pretty fast. So did Vivian. TJ was having a rougher time. There were twenty-five questions on the page and he was only on number twelve.

TJ glanced at my completed paper. "How'd you finish so fast?"

"It's easy," I said. "Want me to show you?"

"Sure."

After a few minutes, TJ had the ratios down. He was a quick learner.

On our way back to Mrs. Field's class, TJ spun around to face me. I quickly held up my hands to protect my snout.

"Thanks for clearing up that ratio stuff," he said.

"Anytime," I said. "Are you going to take a swing at my nose again?"

"No. But if I take up boxing and need your honker as a punching bag, I'll let you know."

TJ laughed and walked into the room. I let out a sigh of relief and followed him.

CHAPTER 5

THE HAMSTER TWIST

It didn't take long for my nose to earn some respect.

Right before lunch one day, Mrs. Field gave us a bathroom break. I was in one of the toilet stalls when Jimmy, TJ, and Mumps strolled in to take a leak. I quickly locked the stall door. The last time they caught me here alone, Jimmy threw a lasso made of shoestrings around my nose and led me around like a wild horse.

I peeked through the crack in the door and watched them. Jimmy reached into his pocket and pulled out a live hamster.

"Meet Dumpster," Jimmy said. "He's the meanest assault hamster in the whole world."

"You can't have a pet in school," Mumps said. "You'll get in serious trouble."

"No one's going to find out."

"Doesn't look mean to me," TJ said. "I know how to handle them. I watch the *Hamster Whisperer* every Thursday night on the Rodent Channel." He reached out to stroke Dumpster's fuzzy head and the rodent attacked, tiny sharp teeth lashing into TJ's fingertip.

"EEEOOOWWW!" TJ screamed. "That thing's a menace to society!"

Jimmy pressed a finger to his lips. "Pipe down. The whole school can hear you."

While TJ ran his finger under cold water, my nostrils gathered up a scent. It was black coffee, spearmint Lifesavers, garlic bagel with cream cheese, a hint of ripe body odor—Principal Cyrano. I could smell his bad breath and underarm stink from across town.

The strength of the aroma meant the principal was heading straight for the boys' bathroom. I had two choices: stay hidden in the toilet stall and let Principal Cyrano bust Jimmy or let the guys know he was coming. After all they had put me through, part of me wanted to watch them squirm. But the other part didn't like to watch people get in trouble.

"Principal Cyrano is coming," I said, bursting out of the stall. "He must've heard TJ's scream."

"How do you know, Schnoz?" Jimmy asked.

"I can smell him. Better put Dumpster away."

"Don't tell me what to do. The little guy needs some air."

Principal Cyrano's funky smell grew stronger, so powerful I could taste it. I smacked Jimmy's arm with my nose. Dumpster fell from his hand onto the floor.

"What did you do that for?" Jimmy yelled.

Before Dumpster could scurry away, I grabbed the rodent and shoved him into my front pocket.

The bathroom door swung open and Principal Cyrano appeared.

"What's going on in here?" he asked.

"Uh nothing," Jimmy said.

"Just going to the bathroom before lunch," Mumps added.

27

Dumpster was on the move. He wriggled through a hole in my pocket and scurried down my pant leg. His sharp little claws tickled my skin. I squirmed, twitched, and convulsed, trying to keep from busting up.

Principal Cyrano looked at me, raised one eyebrow. "Andy, is there something wrong with you?"

"He's practicing a new dance we learned in gym class," Jimmy said, coming to my rescue. "It's called the Hamster Twist. Let's show him."

All the guys in the bathroom started bopping around like wild chimps. Except for TJ, who was still running his hand under the tap, moaning over the hamster bite.

"That's enough, boys," Principal Cyrano ordered. "Get to lunch. Now."

When the coast was clear, I plucked Dumpster from my pants and handed him back to Jimmy.

"Schnoz, you're all right," Jimmy said. "I owe you one."

Inside, I beamed. Finally, my nose was good for something other than making people laugh.

CHAPTER 6

COMIC BOOK CLUB

The halls were buzzing the first week of December. Not because of the upcoming Christmas vacation, but because we could sign up for winter after-school clubs. Outside the front office was a big table filled with registration forms for all the different activities.

For the kindergartners and first graders there was Play Dough Club, karate, Reading Club, and Lego Construction Club. The second and third graders got to pick from Drama Club, origami, dance, Gym Games, and Science Club. Fourth and fifth graders chose from Magic Club, Technology Club, Knitting Club, Choir, Fitness Club, or Comic Book Club.

Before school I hovered around the sign-up table, waiting my turn to register. The line was huge. My bus was late, so I ended up in the very back. I really wanted to be in Magic Club. A rumor was going around that members learned how to yank a rabbit out of a hat. With my massive honker, I could hide a rabbit in each nostril and blow everyone's mind!

By the time I made it to the table, all but two clubs were full: Knitting Club and Comic Book Club.

My heart sank. I wasn't into knitting or comics. Still, I grabbed a Comic Book Club registration and took it home for my mom to sign.

The following Monday after school was the first day of clubs. Comic Book Club met once a week in Mr. Colby's room. He was a third-grade teacher and coached the junior varsity basketball team at the high school. When I tramped into the room, only three other kids were there—Jimmy, TJ, and Mumps.

"Well, if ain't Schnoz," Jimmy said, leaning back in his chair, dirty sneakers propped on the desk.

"I hope you like comics," TJ said to me. "We take this club very serious."

24

"Super serious," Mumps added.

The guys had stopped teasing me as much after the hamster incident. Sure, they still called me Schnoz—everyone did—and occasionally Booger Beak, but it wasn't in a mean way like before. We weren't exactly friends or anything, but I was definitely no longer their enemy.

Mr. Colby walked into the room and welcomed us to Comic Book Club. He explained that we'd be reading comics, talking about comics, and writing and drawing our own comics. He pulled out a box from underneath his desk. "I brought these old comics from when I was a kid."

We rummaged through the box. It was filled with comics I had never heard of before—*Archie*, *Jughead*, *Betty and Veronica*, *Richie Rich*, *Chip 'n' Dale*. From the looks on the other guys' faces, they hadn't heard of them either.

Have fun with these comics," Mr. Colby said. "*Richie Rich* was my all-time favorite."

While Jimmy, TJ, and Mumps huddled in the back, I spent the rest of Comic Book Club reading some of Mr. Colby's comics.

He was right. *Richie Rich* was really good.

"Forget this wimpy stuff," I heard Jimmy say. "The next time we meet, I want to read about *real* superheroes."

A minute later, Mr. Colby dismissed us. I had no idea what Jimmy meant by real superheroes, but the possibilities made my nostrils flare.

CHAPTER 7

SUPER SCHNOZ

The next time Comic Book Club met, we had a new member—Vivian Ramirez. She was wearing all black as usual.

"What are you doing here?" Jimmy asked. "Shouldn't you be in the Vampire Lovers Club?"

"Or knitting," Mumps added.

"Ha-ha, very funny," Vivian said. "For your information, I love comics. I wasn't here on the first day was because I had a dentist appointment."

Mr. Colby walked into the room. He was carrying another big cardboard box.

"Vivian!" Mr. Colby said enthusiastically. "I was hoping you'd show up. You're so talented in art. I can't wait to see what comics you come up with."

"Hello, Mr. Colby," Vivian replied. I was starting to notice that all the teachers loved her, from Mrs. Field to Ms. Thurston and now Mr. Colby.

Spread out on a table next Mr. Colby's desk were drawing pads, colored pencils, and the stack of *Archie* and *Richie Rich* comics. He instructed us to grab a pad and pencils.

"Your comic books are only limited by your imaginations," Mr. Colby said. "I want you to think about the story first. Plan it out frame by frame, then start drawing."

"What's in the box?" Jimmy asked.

"Well, I started thinking. Although I enjoyed comics like *Archie* and *Richie Rich* back when I was a kid, they weren't the most popular. I remember most of my friends liking the ones about superheroes. I still had money left in the budget and got a good deal at Sonic's Used Comics downtown."

Mr. Colby dumped the contents of the box onto the table. Vivian, Jimmy, Mumps, and TJ gushed at what was inside. Dozens of old comic books— *Batman, Spider-Man, Fantastic Four, Flash, Thor,*

28

X-Men, Captain America, Silver Surfer, and a bunch of others I had never heard of before. I could tell by their tattered covers and low price that they were ancient. Some of them were as cheap as twenty-five cents!

"These are great, Mr. Colby," Vivian said.

"Awesome!" Mumps said. "Thanks."

"All of my favorites," TJ said. "The golden age of comics. When men had real superpowers—full body elasticity, super strength, mind control, vaporizing beams."

"And don't forget about the superheroines," Vivian said. "Wonder Woman, Super Girl, She-Hulk, and the Invisible Woman could kick some serious butt."

Mr. Colby smiled. "You can work alone or in teams. Understand?"

We nodded.

"Good. I'll be at my desk if you need me." Mr. Colby sat down, grabbed a *Richie Rich* comic, and started reading. Vivian started sketching on her pad right away. Jimmy, Mumps, and TJ grabbed a stack of *Fantastic Four* comics and went back to their desks. I browsed through the collection, trying to find one I liked. One called *Generation X* caught my attention.

"*Generation X is* a spin-off of the *X-Men* published by Marvel way back in the nineties," Vivian said. "It's about a gang of mutant teenagers."

"Wow," Jimmy said to Vivian. "You really know a lot about comics."

"I'll show you my collection someday," she said. "I even have an old Barbie Batgirl doll still in its box. It's worth almost a hundred dollars."

While Vivian and Jimmy discussed the value of comic book memorabilia, I picked up a few issues of *Generation X* and went back to my desk. Before long, I found a character named Skin I could identify with. He possessed an extra six feet of skin that could stretch. Because of the extra skin, he looked like a melted crayon and people made fun of him.

Kind of like me and my nose.

I picked up a pencil and started doodling. I thought the art wasn't very good, but my idea for a comic was genius. It would be about me and my nose, fighting crime and saving the world from the forces of evil.

The first sketch was of a kid that looked like me with a huge nose. He wore a cape, a mask, pointy boots, and tights. When I finished the sketch, I tried to think of a name for my superhero —Nose Boy, the Head Honker, the Mighty Mucus Maker, the Schnozinator. None of them sounded quite right. I scooted from my desk and walked to the pencil sharpener at the front of the room. That's when Jimmy sat up and checked out my drawing.

"This is great!" he said. "TJ, Mumps, check it out."

TJ and Mumps wandered over and howled with laughter.

"A superhero with a huge nose," Jimmy said. "It looks just like Schnoz."

"Give that back," I said, slightly miffed. I had just started drawing and wasn't ready to share it with anyone.

"Schnoz, you have to let me work on this with you," Mumps said. "It's a great idea."

"Way better than the one we're working on," TJ said. "I want to help too."

"Me three," Jimmy said. "We'll call the comic... *Super Schnoz!*"

CHAPTER 8

JANNA, THE SORCERESS OF ALTHORIA

The guys and I spent the entire nine weeks of Comic Book Club drawing *Super Schnoz*. Since Vivian knew so much about comics and was such a good artist, we asked her to help us. She refused and worked on her own comic.

We divided the *Super Schnoz* comic duties. Jimmy and I came up with the story. TJ and Mumps were the artists. The first part of Super Schnoz was about his origin. I suggested the true story of my nose; the doctor mixing up my mom's prenatal vitamins with a steroid for nasal congestion, but the guys said it wasn't dramatic enough. We came up with a tale of how when Michael

Mitchell (the future Super Schnoz) was a fetus, his nuclear scientist father accidently exposed him to toxic waste. The nuclear contact rearranged his molecules and caused Schnoz's nose to grow.

Super Schnoz also has the power of flight and fire. He can fly around and shoot nuclear-fueled, boogery flames from his nose. Super Schnoz learns from a mysterious old man who owns a crystal shop that the evil Doctor Diabolical is responsible for Schnoz's parents' death over a decade ago. Super Schnoz is rabid for revenge.

Doctor Diabolical kidnaps the president's wife and threatens to kill her if the U.S. government doesn't pay a ransom of fifty billion dollars. He destroys the Empire State Building, the subway system, and most of lower Manhattan. His minions ravage the city, looting and impaling innocent victims on street signs. The president calls on Super Schnoz to rescue his wife and destroy the doctor. After an epic showdown in Central Park, Super Schnoz kills the doctor and his minions with a blast from his atomic nose. The president's wife is safe and Super Schnoz becomes a national hero.

"I love it!" Mr. Colby exclaimed when he finished reading. "The drawings and story are excellent. I especially like how you named Doctor Diabolical's second-in-command after me. Great job, boys. Good teamwork."

Vivian's comic blew us all away. Her artwork was amazing. It was full-color and looked like she had just bought it from a store. The title was the *Unicorn Avenger* starring Janna, the Sorceress of Althoria. It was page after page of Janna riding a magical-winged unicorn and fighting the evil Bloborg and his army of zombie gargoyles. The three main gargoyles—Klutzo, Mutzo, and Butzo—looked a lot like Jimmy, TJ, and Mumps.

"I'm speechless, Vivian," Mr. Colby said. "Your work is stunning. Isn't it, boys?"

We nodded.

"How did you come up with such an awesome story?" Jimmy asked.

Vivian shrugged. "Don't know. It just popped into my head."

"You're a real artist," TJ said. "Maybe you can work for Marvel or DC when you get older."

34

Mr. Colby packed up his comic books. "You all are real artists," he said. "I think all four of you have a real future in the superhero biz."

"Maybe we can do a comic together," Jimmy suggested. "We can team up Super Schnoz and Janna."

"It's just like that old issue of *Batman* when he teams up with Wonder Woman to find out who kidnapped Robin," Mumps added.

"I'd love to," Vivian said. "But I don't think you could afford my fee. I'm pretty expensive."

We all laughed and helped pack things up.

"Hey, Schnoz," Jimmy said. "My birthday's next weekend and I'm having a party. Want to come?"

"Okay," I said, trying to sound as chill as possible. But inside I was exploding with joy.

We had had so much fun together creating *Super Schnoz*, so I guess the invitation meant we were friends. And I hadn't had a real friend since I moved to New Hampshire.

CHAPTER 9

HOMER BY A NOSE

Jimmy's birthday was on the seventeenth, St. Patrick's Day. It was a pretty warm day for March. The snow was almost melted and tulip bulbs were popping out of the ground.

When my mom dropped me off in front of Jimmy's house, I saw a familiar face sitting on the porch of a house directly across the street.

It was Vivian, dressed in all black.

"What are you doing?" I asked her.

"Sitting on my porch," she said. "What does it look like?"

"I didn't know you and Jimmy were neighbors. Are you coming to his party?"

"Can't. I have a guitar lesson. I'm a bass player."
She stood up, zipped up her black windbreaker,
and went into the house.

I bounded up the cement steps to Jimmy's front
door. Since I was holding his present with both
hands, I rang the bell with the tip of my nose.

Jimmy's mom answered the door. When she
saw me standing there, her eyes grew as wide as
paper plates. She just stared at my nose, like the
gigantic appendage in the middle of my face was
hypnotizing her or something.

"You must be...uh...Schn...I mean...Andy,"
she said.

I nodded my nose and she invited me inside.
Mumps and TJ were already there.

"Schnoz!" they yelled in unison.

Since baseball season was just around the
corner, we went outside and played a couple
games of Wiffle ball. Jimmy and I played against TJ
and Mumps. They beat us ten to one the first game
because my giant nose kept messing up my swing.
I struck out every time. The next game was more of
the same, until Jimmy came up with an idea.

"Schnoz, they're killing us by five runs and it's only the third inning," Jimmy said. "Ditch the bat and use your nose."

"What do you mean?" I asked.

"Use your nose as a bat. You might do better."

I shrugged my shoulders and said okay. Jimmy had smacked a double into the weeds behind his house. It was my turn to hit. Mumps and TJ busted up laughing when they saw me standing there without a bat.

"Schnoz, don't tell me you're hitting with just your nose," Mumps said.

"That's exactly what he's doing," Jimmy announced.

"He'll strike out for sure!" TJ shouted from the outfield.

"Just pitch," I said. Mumps wound up and whizzed a zinger right past my honker. The rush of wind from the ball made my nostrils flare like a whale's blowhole.

"Swing next time!" Jimmy yelled. "That was a perfect pitch!"

The next pitch came right for my nose. I closed

my eyes and swung my honker with all my might. The ball cracked against my left nostril and flew into the air. TJ ran back to catch it, but slipped in the mud. The ball landed in the lawn next door. Jimmy scored and I rounded the bases for my first home run.

I hit four more dingers and we won the game eleven to seven. When it was time for cake, Jimmy carried me inside on his shoulders like we'd just won the Little League World Series.

CHAPTER 10

HIDE-AND-SNIFF

My nose sometimes came in handy for things other than smelling, hitting home runs, and inspiring comic books. I also used it to block a teacher's sight line when Jimmy, Mumps, or TJ wanted to sleep in class, draw comics instead of read, or just goof off. A simple flare of my nostrils was enough to keep at least one of my new friends hidden from view.

One day Mrs. Field pulled a pop quiz on us. It was about colonial history. Jimmy asked me to do something about it. I snorted a tablespoon of black pepper and sneezed so hard the fire alarms went off.

No pop quiz.

My special gift also created a new game on the playground. Instead of hide-and-seek, we played hide-and-sniff. I was always the sniffer; my friends were the hiders. The game was simple. Kids smuggled gross things from home, hid them on school grounds, and I'd sniff them out. When I found everything, I determined the smelliest item and crowned a winner. That meant the fouler the stench, the better odds to win. Jimmy made a fortune taking bets.

Kids hid sandwich baggies full of fish guts, their dad's smelly socks, cat litter clumps, used diapers, moldy mac and cheese, rotten leftover egg salad, and dozens of other malodorous mixtures meant to offend mere mortals.

But not me, I inhaled everything they threw at me.

Jimmy raised his bet-taking notebook in the air, "Schnoz has to find seven skanky things in less than ten minutes!" he shouted, "On your mark...get set...go!"

I was off. Nose to the ground, butt in the air, hot on the scent.

"Look at him go," I heard TJ say. "That nose of his is amazing. He really does have a superpower!"

"Go, Super Schnoz!" Jimmy hollered.

The crowd picked up on Jimmy's call. All I heard were shouts of "Super Schnoz! Super Schnoz! Super Schnoz!"

The first thing I dug up was the arch support for an old sneaker. It was stinky, but not nearly enough to win. The second item, which I sniffed out under the climbing wall, was a plastic bag filled with dog poop—definitely a contender.

I found the other five objects in quick succession. There was a maggoty hunk of decaying bologna under the teeter-totter, a partially decomposed roadkill chipmunk behind the backstop on the baseball field, a pair of skid-mark-stained underwear buried under a pile of leaves, a container of reeking pond scum wedged between two big rocks, and a clipping of greasy black hair stuffed in a thorny bush. A note attached claimed the hair was from Kenny Walters, the grimiest kid in school.

"Who's the winner?" a third-grader asked when I joined the crowd. "I got all my lunch money on the dead chipmunk."

"No way," said Vivian. "It's the dog poop. That's the most disgusting thing ever."

"Both of you are wrong," I said. "The winner is...the maggoty hunk of bologna!"

Half the crowd cheered, the other half groaned. Jimmy held out his wallet, collecting his winnings.

As we tramped back into the building after recess, another strange scent wafted in the air, one I had never smelled before. My nostrils spread wide. The hairs inside my nose bristled with excitement. I inhaled deeply. It was a delicious mixture of dead rodent, raw sewage, and stale fart.

But the other kids in school reacted very differently to the odor.

Some nearly passed out. Others lost their lunch in the hallway.

Principal Cyrano's panicked voice blasted through the intercom. "Evacuate the school! This is not a drill! Everyone must leave the building immediately!"

CHAPTER 11

EVACUATION

Three hundred kids and twenty-seven teachers poured out of the school. Two police cars, an ambulance, a news crew, and a big yellow hazmat truck whipped into the parking lot. Men wearing gas masks charged into the building.

A reporter spoke into a camera. "Something is rotten in the town of Denmark," she said in a perfect TV voice. "A foul, offensive odor is permeating James F. Durante Elementary School. It's described as a fishy, raw sewage smell that made several children and teachers ill earlier today. Here is eleven-year-old Vivian Ramirez with a comment."

"I couldn't breathe," Vivian said into the microphone. "The smell is just so disgusting. It's really scaring me."

"The source of the smell has yet to be determined," the reporter continued. "A private company, ECU—Environmental Clean Up, Inc., is in the school right now, conducting air quality tests."

The reporter moved on to an ECU representative. "What exactly does your company do?" she asked.

"Our mission is to solve environmental problems with scientifically sound results and to maintain compliance that ensures the safety and health of all individuals," the representative said.

While the reporter jabbered on, interviewing other kids and teachers, I tiptoed away from the crowd and slipped back into the school.

The smell was powerful. I crept up the second-grade hall, past the custodian's closet, and into the teachers' lounge. The funky fragrance seeped into everything, so much that it was hard for me to determine its source. It could have been anything—a ruptured sewer line, a clogged-up poopy toilet, or the greasy taco meat the cafeteria ladies served up for lunch.

I heard a deep voice bellow from down the hall. "Follow me into the teachers' lounge. We need to talk."

It was Principal Cyrano. If he caught me inside the school when we were supposed to evacuate, I would be in serious trouble. I dashed behind the copy machine.

I was perfectly concealed, except for my nose. It was sticking out from the side of the copy machine like the rudder of a boat.

The door flew open. I prayed the principal wouldn't notice my snout.

"What's the verdict?" Principal Cyrano asked through a gas mask.

"We've unearthed very high levels of methane, butane, and propane. That could be to blame," said a woman's muffled voice. "But we also have to consider other sources, like dead rodents, soil contamination, and gas line issues."

"How long will it take to determine the cause?"

"It could be days, weeks, maybe even months. Until then, no students will be allowed into the building."

"But where are we going to house them? If we don't open this school soon, our kids will be in class all summer. Kiss vacation good-bye for everyone."

"That, sir, is your problem."

I heard the door close and footsteps disappear down the hallway. Principal Cyrano and the woman were gone. Just as I was about to crawl from behind the copy machine, the door opened again. My heart pounded in my chest. I was sure

48

the whole world could hear it.

"The principal is clueless," a hushed voice said. I knew right away it was the same woman who had been talking to Principal Cyrano only moments before.

"Good," a man's gravelly voice croaked. "That imbecile doesn't realize he has a gold mine sitting right under his feet and I want to keep it that way. How long will this phase of the operation take?"

"I'd say two or three months before the government officially condemns the property."

"Perfect. Get this school shut down and ECU will purchase it for a song."

The door closed. I was alone, trying to digest what I had just heard. No summer vacation!

I inhaled the luscious stench, filing the stink inside my mental smell library, and rushed back outside.

CHAPTER 12

SUMMER SCHOOL

The next day we were back in school, but not at James F. Durante Elementary.

We were in the high school auditorium for a big assembly.

It was the only place in town that could fit three hundred kids.

"This is a challenging situation for everyone," Principal Cyrano announced. "I just received confirmation from our superintendent that we will temporarily move to the old school across town while the environmental company cleans up Durante Elementary. However, since the old school has sat vacant for three years, it will take the maintenance department at least two weeks to get the building ready for students. After today there will be no classes until the old school is ready to go."

A cheer went up from the kids.

Principal Cyrano clapped his hands, quieting everyone down. "However," he continued, "the Department of Education says that students must complete one hundred and seventy-four days of quality instruction. That means every missed day of school must be made up during the summer months."

Every kid in the auditorium groaned. This information wasn't new to me, so I just rolled my eyes and flared my nostrils.

"No way!" Jimmy said. "My butt will not be in school one day past June seventh. Period!"

"I'm going to Camp Noogiewagga for two weeks at the end of June," TJ said. "It's the first year I can do sleepover."

"My family's going to Cape Cod," Mumps said. "If we're still in school, I'll miss it."

As for me, my summer plans included a self-guided odor tour of the tri-county region. Just me, my nose, my bike, and a snoot full of smelly things.

"Nothing we can do about now," I said. "Let's just hope they find the source of the smell and clean it up."

Mumps opened his backpack and pulled out his most prized possession—issue 232 of *Fantastic Four* from 1981 in mint condition. He had bought it a year ago at a comic book convention for thirteen dollars and fifty cents—his whole life savings—and carried it with him everywhere.

The front cover was Mister Fantastic, the Invisible Woman, Thing, and the Human Torch shooting into the sky on fire with some devil-looking creature in the background. It was in way better shape than the comics Mr. Colby showed us in Comic Book Club.

It didn't mean much to me, but to Mumps, TJ, and Jimmy, the comic was like an ancient holy relic.

"This issue's a collector's item," Mumps said, slowly peeling the pages out of its protective plastic cover.

"That's what I want to be when I grow up," TJ said. "Part of a superhero team."

"Me too," Jimmy said. "Wouldn't it be great if we could do that right now?"

"Totally awesome," Mumps said dreamily.

The guys stared at the comic, carefully turning the pages. The artwork was pretty good. I liked Mister Fantastic's ability to stretch his body into different shapes.

"Wouldn't it be funny if my nose stretched into weird shapes, like Mister Fantastic?" I asked.

Jimmy looked at me. His eyes lit up. "You can be a superhero."

"What are you talking about?"

"That nose of yours. It has superpowers."

"Jimmy's right," TJ said. "Anybody who can sniff out dog poop from over a hundred yards away has a true gift. With your schnoz, we can discover the source of the smell. The kids at school will love us."

"You're Super Schnoz," Mumps said. "Just like in our comic book—only you're real!"

TJ howled, pumping his fists in the air, chanting, "Super Schnoz! Super Schnoz! Super Schnoz!"

I hadn't told anyone about sneaking into the school during the evacuation partly because I was in denial about what I'd overheard in the teachers' lounge and partly because I didn't want to get in trouble for breaking the rules. I guess now was time to spill the beans.

"Remember when that reporter was interviewing everyone the day were evacuated?" I said.

"Sure," Jimmy said. "I made it on TV!"

"Well, while you were getting your fifteen

minutes of fame, I snuck back inside the school to investigate."

Mumps slapped me on the back. "Everyone knows you have a nose for trouble."

"I know smells. And the smell inside that school was nothing I had ever sniffed before. I tried huffing out where it was coming from, but it was too overpowering, even for me."

"I don't believe it, Schnoz," Jimmy said. "Nothing's too strong for your nose. Let's start hatching our plan at my house this afternoon. What do you say?"

I shrugged. It sounded okay to me, but I had no idea what they were planning.

"Schnoz, you'll need a costume," Mumps said. "All the greats have a mask, cape, tights, pointy boots, just like in our comic book."

"And a big Schnoz emblem plastered across the chest!" Jimmy added.

"Let's ask Vivian to design it," I said. "She's the best artist I know."

The guys all nodded in agreement. Someone tapped me on the shoulder. I turned around and saw Vivian. She was sitting in the row behind ours.

"I'll do it," she said. "And I won't even charge you."

"Great," said Jimmy. "My older sister wants to be a fashion designer. She showed me how to use her sewing machine. I can totally make your costume."

Super Schnoz—it was a great name for a comic book. Could it be a great name for a real superhero too? Could I save summer vacation for all my friends? How would I look in a cape and tights?

I was about to find out.

CHAPTER 13

IT'S A BIRD...IT'S A PLANE...
IT'S SUPER SCHNOZ!

Vivian's design was perfect. It was a jet black, one-piece suit with a flowing blue cape and a big pair of black pointy boots. Her drawing looked just like me. She had a big nose in three-quarter profile splashed across the chest and the letters *SS* written on the back of the cape.

"Are you sure you can make this, Jimmy?" Vivian asked.

"No problem," Jimmy said and went right to work.

Jimmy wasn't lying. He was a whiz with his sister's sewing machine. In less than an hour, he had stitched together a cape and long sleeve shirt.

The only things he couldn't make were the tights. I acquired those compliments of his sister too. Jimmy swiped a pair of black dance pants from her dresser drawer.

Since Vivian was the artist, painting the Super Schnoz emblem on the shirt was her responsibility.

"The nostrils aren't big enough," TJ said. "You gotta make them huge."

"It's not my fault," Vivian fired back. "Schnoz keeps squirming around. Models are supposed to sit still."

I stopped fidgeting, turned profile, and took a deep breath. "Hurry up. Not moving is next to impossible."

Ten minutes later it was over. She had drawn a perfect image of my nose in profile on the shirt.

"Schnoz, try on everything," Vivian ordered.

I went into the bathroom and closed the door. The costume fit like a freshly laundered sock, from the black shirt and tights right down to the blue cape and Super Schnoz logo. But I refused to wear pointy black boots. My old sneakers would be just fine.

"It's a bird, it's a plane, it's Super Schnoz!" I

cried and leaped from the bathroom, chest puffed out, nose held high.

The guys and Vivian rolled on the floor, laughing so hard tears streamed down their cheeks.

"Perfect!" TJ squealed.

"Better than perfect," Mumps said, "It's Schnozalicious!"

"Let's go in my backyard," Jimmy said. "I want to take some pictures."

It was a sunny, breezy, chilly April afternoon. Wind whipped through the trees, showering us with fallen leaves. I didn't have a jacket, but the black tights and cape kept me warm.

"Stand next to the fence," Jimmy said. "And pose like a superhero."

"What do you mean?" I said.

"You know, stick out your arms like you're ready to fly or something."

Mumps straightened out my cape. "It would be so awesome if you could really fly."

"Awesome for you, maybe," I replied. "I'm afraid of heights. Just climbing the slide freaks me out."

I leaned over slightly and stretched my arms, nose pointing skyward. "How's this for a pose?"

Jimmy flashed me a thumbs-up and snapped some pictures.

That's when a huge gust of wind blasted through his backyard. The cold air shot up my nostrils and inflated them like two giant parachutes. My heart dropped into my stomach, my toes lifted off the ground, and my cape fluttered in the breeze.

I was flying!

CHAPTER 14

THE NOT-RIGHT BROTHERS...AND VIVIAN

Well, I wasn't really flying. I was floating, like a kite or hot air balloon. As the wind lifted me higher, I saw the inside of Jimmy's second floor bedroom window, then the cracked tiles of his roof, the telephone wires, treetops. The town of Denmark stretched out below me like a miniature world.

"Help!" I screamed. "Get me down from here!"

A gigantic crow answered with a loud squawk. It flapped beside me then landed on the bridge of my nose. Something warm and wet dribbled down my cheek.

Bird poop.

The crow preened its feathers. One fell out and

tickled my nose, and I sneezed. The expulsion of air was so powerful it propelled me halfway across town.

And that's how I learned to control my flight pattern.

To fly faster, I inhaled and exhaled deeply from my nose. The harder I huffed the faster I flew. Landing was just as easy. When I wanted to descend, I closed one nostril with a finger, breathed very lightly, and drifted to the ground as daintily as a dandelion seed.

"Schnoz...really...flying," Mumps stammered when I landed back in the yard.

"You really are a superhero," TJ said, a hint of awe in his voice.

"I am completely freaking out right now," Vivian said.

Jimmy tapped the big Super Schnoz logo on my chest. "You, my friend, are the greatest thing since the Wright Brothers."

"More like the Not-Right Brothers," I said.

All four of them laughed at my joke.

"Have you always been able to fly?" Mumps asked.

"Of course not," I said. "The wind just inflated my nostrils and lifted me off the ground."

"Is this the first time your nose ever filled up with air and sent you into the sky?" Vivian asked.

I nodded. What did she think? My snout was an alien ship from another planet or something?

"Schnoz flew because of a very a basic scientific principal," TJ said. "Warm air rises in cooler air."

"What makes you such an expert?" Jimmy asked.

TJ grabbed a stick and drew a picture of a big balloon in the dirt. "My Uncle Grady is a hot air balloon fanatic. He told me all about how they work. Hot air is lighter than cooler air. Schnoz's two massive nose holes are like mini hot air balloons. The cold air blew into his nostrils, warmed, and caused him to float. Simple."

"So you're saying I'm some kind of human hot air balloon," I said.

"Exactly." TJ said. "With your power to fly, we can be a famous crime-fighting team like the Fantastic Four. Solve mysteries and beat up bad guys."

"Super Schnoz and the Not-Right Brothers!" Jimmy howled. "You're the superhero and we're the support team."

"Ahem," Vivian grunted, clearing her throat.

"I mean, Super Schnoz, the Not-Right Brothers, and Vivian."

"Awesome!" Mumps added. "We can work the computers and GPS satellites, and intercept and decode messages from our archenemy."

"But we don't have an archenemy," I said.

Jimmy dropped his smile and stared at me. "Whoever or whatever is causing that smell in our school is enemy number one as far as I'm concerned. If we don't discover the source, say good-bye to summer vacation."

Jimmy was right. I had been planning my July odor tour for months. Summer school meant no new smells for my scent dictionary.

"We have to lay down some ground rules first," I said.

"Like what?" TJ asked.

"Like my secret identity. No one knows Clark Kent is Superman, Peter Parker is Spider-Man, or that Principal Krupp is Captain Underpants. My true identity must remain top secret or this whole thing will blow up."

"He's right," Jimmy said. "We have to promise never to reveal Schnoz as Super Schnoz or that we're the Not-Right Brothers."

"Then we'll need to disguise Schnoz's nose," TJ said. "People in town will take one look at that snout and recognize him right away."

Vivian paced around the yard, thinking. "Got it!" she exclaimed and raced to her house. She returned five minutes later, holding a bundle of feathers.

"What's that?" I asked.

"It's a Mardi Gras mask with a beak," Vivian said. "My parents went on a trip to New Orleans last year. They brought home a bunch of masks as souvenirs."

The mask had red, green, and orange feathers with a large silver beak. Black feathers accented the eyeholes to make them stand out.

"Try it on," Jimmy said.

I slipped the rubber bands over my ears and pulled the mask over my face. The beak fit perfectly

over my nose while still leaving room to flare my nostrils for flight.

"I love it," I said.

"Awesome!" TJ squealed. "The beak totally disguises your nose. You can't tell it's you!"

"You look like some freaky bird," Mumps said.

I took off the mask and pointed to the tip of my nose. The others bent over until all of our noses were touching.

"On the count of three," I said. "One, two, three,"

"SUPER SCHNOZ!" we all screamed.

The pact was complete.

Our vow of secrecy sealed with a sniff.

CHAPTER 15

DISASTER SITE

The third week of April was Spring Break. That meant no classes for seven glorious days! Principal Cyrano wanted to cancel the break because of the school situation, but the teachers already had the time off written in their contract.

Some kids went to special day camps at the YMCA for the week; others hopped on a plane for a Disney vacation with their parents. The Not-Right Brothers and I spent the time off riding our bicycles, casing Durante Elementary. Vivian couldn't come because she had to visit her sick grandmother for a couple of days.

We pedaled up and down the street, checking

things out. I didn't want to attract attention, so I didn't wear my Super Schnoz costume. A tall metal fence topped with razor wire surrounded the school property. Armed men with snarling dogs guarded the place. We watched as a fleet of bulldozers, forklifts, backhoes, drilling machines, and other construction equipment so specialized we didn't know what they were for ripped apart our school. Dozens of workers crawled around the school like a colony of ants. They wore hard hats and safety glasses, poring over construction blueprints. The sounds of jackhammers, loud whistles, and excavators blasted in our ears.

We parked our bikes behind the baseball field across from the school. Jimmy brought a pair of binoculars so we could take turns spying on the action.

"Seems like a lot of security and equipment just to uncover a bad smell," I said.

"You got that right," Jimmy said.

"What should we do?" Mumps asked.

TJ pulled out his big camera with a long distance lens. "I need to get some reconnaissance photos so we can study them later." He spent the rest of the afternoon secretly snapping pictures of the school's perimeter.

The next day was the most dramatic of all. From our hiding place behind the baseball field, we watched a convoy of flatbed trucks loaded with hundreds of rubber hoses wheel into the parking lot. Then a bunch of oversized-load trucks carrying massive storage containers rumbled inside.

"This is crazy," I said. "Our school looks like a disaster site."

"Whatever's inside must be really toxic," Mumps said.

I stood up, lifted my nose, and sniffed the air. "Something toxic or something fishy," I said.

"What do you mean?" Jimmy asked.

"They have millions of dollars worth of equipment in there. And they're employing dozens of construction workers and scientists. This is a huge operation—all to clean up a dinky elementary school in the middle of New Hampshire."

"Schnoz is right," TJ said, snapping more pictures with his camera.

I grabbed the binoculars and focused in on the school. I saw more trucks enter the grounds, followed by what looked like an army tank. Then, out of the corner of my eye, I saw a bicycle slowly pedaling down the street. I zoomed in for a closer look.

"It's Vivian," I said out loud.

"I thought she was still at her grandmother's house," Mumps said.

I shrugged. "Maybe she came back early."

"What's she doing?" Jimmy asked.

"Just riding her bicycle slowly up and down the street by the school, the part that isn't blocked off."

A dog barked behind us, and a man's gruff voice called out, "What are you kids doing here?"

We turned and saw an ECU guard. He was dressed in an all-black security uniform, carrying a walkie-talkie and holding a snarling, vicious-looking rottweiler.

"You kids don't belong here," the guard said.

"We just came to play baseball," I said.

"This whole area is off-limits. Don't you

know there's a dangerous odor coming from that school?"

My friends and I just stood there, not knowing what to do. This was the chance I had been waiting for. I wanted to ask an ECU employee what was really going on inside our school.

"Why do you need all those trucks?" I asked. "And what are those rubber hoses for?"

"It's none of your business!" the guard barked. "All you need to know is that we're searching for toxic materials. Our number one concern is for your safety. Now get out of here before I turn my dog loose."

We packed up our stuff and high-tailed it out of there. None of us said a word until we were almost to Jimmy's house.

"That was close," Mumps said.

"What do we do now?" Jimmy asked.

A park bench sat in a little patch of green space near Jimmy's house. I plopped down and tried to take in the events over the last few weeks— the smell, the evacuation, the possibility of no summer vacation, our school that was now a disaster site. I was angry and knew that I had to do something about it.

"We're superheroes," I said. "Let's go back to our secret hideout and plan our attack."

"But we don't have a secret hideout," Mumps said.

"Then it's time we got one."

CHAPTER 16

THE NOSTRIL

Batman had the Bat Cave, the Fantastic Four had the Baxter Building, Super Schnoz, the Not-Right Brothers, and Vivian had the Nostril.

It was really just an old shed in Jimmy's backyard. After we hauled out all the bicycles, lawn stuff, and rusty gasoline cans, it became the nerve center of our mystery-solving, crime-fighting operation.

Communication, comfort, and secrecy were of prime importance. The communication part came from four high-power walkie-talkies and TJ's laptop with wireless Internet connection. Comfort came from some junky folding chairs and a stained, musty couch from Jimmy's basement. Secrecy was a combination lock on the shed door to keep out nosy intruders.

But there was a catch.

Jimmy was the only one who knew the combination. That way if an evil villain captured any of us and slipped a truth serum inside our drink, only Jimmy would know the numbers. That's why keeping Jimmy safe at all times was extremely important.

Every morning we headed straight for the Nostril to plan our attack.

TJ flipped open his laptop, connected his digital camera, and downloaded dozens of photos.

"These are the reconnaissance photos I took of the school," he said. "As you all know, ECU is guarding the place like Fort Knox. It's going to be wicked hard getting inside without detection."

I carefully studied the photos.

"They're hiding something," Jimmy said. "I just know it."

"I agree," Vivian said. "Why would there be such tight security if it was only a burst sewer line or a bunch of dead rats causing the smell?"

That's when I remembered the conversation I'd heard on the day of the evacuation.

"Remember I told you about sneaking back into the school the day of the smell?" I said.

Vivian and the Not-Right Brothers nodded.

"When I was hiding behind the copy machine in the teachers' lounge, a man and woman came in and talked about gold mines under their feet and condemning the school. I didn't pay much attention then because I was too worried about summer vacation."

"Who were they?" Mumps asked.

"Not sure. I didn't see their faces."

"Gold schmold," Jimmy said. "I only care about discovering the source of that smell and reopening the school."

"Just look at these pictures," TJ said. "It's as plain as the nose on Schnoz's face. We're not walking through the front door."

I grabbed the mouse from TJ's laptop and zoomed in on one of the photos. "Look closer," I said. "There's a glaring hole in ECU's security."

"Where?" Jimmy said. "I don't see anything."

"What do you see on the roof?"

"Nothing."

"That's exactly the point. We're not walking through the front door. I'm flying over the school and landing on the roof."

CHAPTER 17

STORM CLOUDS

The next Saturday, Jimmy's mom gave him permission to have a sleepover. We all brought our toothbrushes and pajamas, but no one was planning on getting much sleep. When night fell and Jimmy's parents went to bed, Super Schnoz and the Not-Right Brothers flew into action.

I tied my cape around my neck, slipped on the Mardi Gras mask, and met the guys inside the Nostril. TJ had his laptop open, checking out the weather and wind conditions for my midnight flight.

"Where's Vivian?" I asked. "She was supposed to sneak out and meet us."

"Maybe she got busted," Mumps said.

"We can't wait for her," TJ said. "The National Weather Service radar says a storm is approaching from the west. It will be here in two hours or so. What do you think, Schnoz?"

"Two hours is plenty of time for me to land on the school and scope out the situation."

"There may be lightning. That could be extremely dangerous if you're in the air."

"You could sizzle like a piece of bacon," Mumps added.

Jimmy closed the lid of the laptop, powering it down. "Forget about this stuff," he said. "We have to do it tonight, storm and all. My mom only lets me have a sleepover once a month. We can't wait another month to see what's going on inside the school."

"Schnoz might not be able to fly in severe weather conditions," TJ argued. "What if he lands on the roof okay, then can't lift off because of the rain? Or worse yet, the wind speed is so strong it blows him all the way to Boston."

I stepped outside, licked my finger, and held it in the air. "The wind feels like it's blowing at around twenty miles per hour."

TJ shot Jimmy a dirty look. "That's exactly what the Doppler radar said on my computer before someone rudely shut it down. The closer the storm gets, the faster the wind. It could double and maybe even triple in velocity."

"He has to do it," Jimmy pleaded. "There's no choice."

I took a deep breath and stared into the night sky. Storm clouds billowed, erasing the stars and moon. The wind whipped through the trees. The mission would be dangerous, but our plan seemed solid. I turned to my comrades.

"Let's get this nose in the air, Not-Right Brothers," I said, sliding a walkie-talkie into my belt. "We're wasting precious seconds."

The boys moved into position inside the Nostril, TJ monitoring the weather and communications, Mumps and Jimmy waiting outside to see if I needed help with liftoff. I stood in the center of the lawn, away from the trees and house so nothing could interfere.

A gust of wind shot in my direction. I inhaled deeply, and my nostrils flared like the wings of a giant prehistoric pterodactyl. I was off the ground, drifting effortlessly over the house, above the town of Denmark, toward the school.

And that's when I saw a UH-60L Black Hawk military helicopter, armed and dangerous, rise from a pad in the school parking lot making a beeline in my direction.

CHAPTER 18

DANG TURKEY BUZZARD

The Black Hawk was on me fast. It was so close I could see the whites of the pilot's eyes. I plugged my right nostril with my finger and banked sharply to the left, bringing me within feet of the helicopter's four-bladed rotating wings. Just as they were about to hack me to pieces, the helicopter turned suddenly to the right, missing me by inches.

"Nothing but a dang turkey buzzard!" I heard the pilot yell above the whine of the wings, and the Black Hawk flew out of sight.

A wave of relief swept over me. Thanks to the mask, the pilot had mistaken me for a bird. With the attack copter threat out of the way, I continued my descent to the school roof. The wind had picked up slightly and a light, misty rain began to fall. I lowered my nose, lifted my rear, and made a soft landing onto the asphalt roof.

I plucked the walkie-talkie out of my belt and contacted home base. "Nostril, Nostril, come in," I whispered. "Super Schnoz has landed. Can you read me, Nostril?"

"Reading you loud and clear, Super Schnoz," TJ said on the other end.

"I've landed undetected. How's the latest weather report?"

"Not so good. Storm's getting closer. Reports of damaging high winds and lightning."

"I'll work fast. Over and out."

I hung up the walkie-talkie and assessed the situation. Armed guards with large dogs roamed the perimeter. Spotlights sliced the school grounds. I stumbled around in the wet darkness, searching for the roof hatch the custodian, Mr. Tobey, used when he worked on the roof. I didn't get ten yards before I found it. I gripped the handle and tugged with all my might. It didn't budge. Too bad my superpower wasn't strength instead of smell.

The only option was painfully clear: I'd have to risk scaling down the side of the building and finding a way inside from ground level.

The rain came down harder. Lightning flared in the distance, followed by cracks of thunder. I moved to the edge of the building and looked down. A dog snarled and a harsh beam of a flashlight blinded me. I froze like a stone gargoyle, my cape fluttering in the wind.

Two armed guards stared at me from below.

"What's that thing on the roof?" one of them called out.

"Don't know," the other said, scratching his head. "Looks to me like a dang turkey buzzard."

"Shoo, you ugly bird, or I'll sic my mutt on you!"

The men laughed and disappeared around the side of the building.

When everything was clear, I inflated my nostrils and wafted gently to the ground.

CHAPTER 19

THE GATES OF SMELL

I may have been a turkey buzzard on the roof, but on the ground I was just an eleven-year-old kid in a cape. Who knew what would happen if one of the guards busted me? I scurried along the side of the building, away from the dogs, guards, and spotlights, searching for a crack in their security.

It didn't take me long to find one.

The door at the end of the first-grade wing that we used for recess didn't shut properly. The latch always caught, leaving the door slightly ajar. Jimmy and I had discovered it one Saturday afternoon when we stopped by the school to collect some new smells for my scent dictionary. We had sneaked inside and roamed the empty school.

I slowly creaked open the door and stepped inside. Instantly, the smell hit me like a rubber dodgeball in the face. It was strong, deliciously tantalizing. A wonderful combination of bad breath, poopy bathroom, body odor, and a million other stinky smells rolled into one.

Loud footsteps echoed in my direction. I dashed inside Mrs. Ferotte's room and hid behind her desk. The door opened, and I could smell wet dog and leather boots. It was a gas-mask-wearing guard. His German shepherd was panting heavily. I quickly started licking myself like a cat, trying to remove my scent so the dog wouldn't pick it up.

It worked. The classroom door shut, and the guard and his dog disappeared back down the hall.

I crawled from my hiding place, my nose leading me in the direction of the smell. Although the scent permeated every crack and crevice of the school, I soon discovered the epicenter—the school gymnasium.

A team of guards stood at each entrance, but I knew a different way. The stage connected the music room and the gym, so I tiptoed toward the art and music hallway. There wasn't a guard in sight, so I opened the music door and slipped inside.

I peeked around the red velvet curtain. A huge pit spiraling deep into the earth had replaced the gym floor. Scientists wearing gas masks and white lab coats hovered like bees in a hive. Dozens of

large hoses snaked into the pit, sucking out barrel after barrel of black, goopy liquid.

With every slurp of the hoses, the smell grew a thousand times more powerful. The black liquid was the source of the stink!

I had to see what was inside the pit. Hanging on pegs to my right were several gas masks, security badges, clipboards, and white lab coats. I grabbed a set and slipped them on. I hid my Mardi Gras mask on the stage and pulled on the gas mask. An extra-large size barely fit over my nose.

Pretending like I was scribbling stuff down on the clipboard, I walked over to the pit and peered inside. What I saw nearly blew my nose. The pit seemed bottomless. Flames crackled deep inside the core of the earth and gurgling, boiling black ooze simmered and popped in smoky stink bubbles.

I shivered inside; my blood grew cold. It was like something from a horror movie—only this was real life. I knew without a doubt what terrible sight I was gazing upon.

The Gates of Smell.

CHAPTER 20

MISSION STATEMENT

A bony finger tapped my shoulder. "You look lost. Are you one of the new scientists?"

I turned to see one of the lab-coated scientists standing behind me. He was wearing a gas mask so I couldn't see his face, but I recognized the voice. It belonged to the mysterious man from the teachers' lounge the day we evacuated the school.

"Uh...sure," I muttered, lowering my voice to sound more grown-up.

"Then you need to be in orientation. It's in the school library. ECU policy forbids any new hires from the Pumping Floor without first having a thorough understanding of our operation. Understand?"

"Sorry," I mumbled then hurried down the hall before he noticed I was just a kid.

I whisked past security and headed for the library. When I got there I didn't recognize the place. Gone were the books, magazines, and computer terminals. Replacing them were Smart Boards and huge diagrams of Earth's core and detailed maps of the school and town of Denmark.

Several new scientists in white coats sat at worktables, fiddling with their pens, waiting for the meeting to begin. I grabbed the only empty seat next to a scientist who was only an inch or two taller than me and wearing a gas mask like

everyone else. Long black hair stuck out from under the helmet.

A tall woman with short blond hair stood up from one of the tables and addressed the room. "I am Dr. Louise Buggingham," she said. "ECU's Senior Vice President of Scientific Study."

I instantly recognized the woman's voice from when I had hid behind the copy machine the day of the evacuation.

"You have been chosen for several reasons," Buggingham continued. "For your impeccable scientific credentials, your commitment to ECU's mission, and your ability to keep your mouths shut. This is a top-secret operation that will make us all very, very wealthy."

A ripple of excitement stirred through the crowd. I heard a scientist at another table hum the word *ka-ching*. The others stood and gave Buggingham a standing ovation—except for me and the scientist sitting next to me.

Buggingham flicked on the Smart Board. ECU's mission statement flashed on the screen.

Our mission is to solve environmental problems

with scientifically sound results and to maintain compliance that ensures the safety and health of all individuals.

I had heard this before. Their mission statement was exactly what an ECU representative told the reporter the day they evacuated us!

"This is what we tell the general public," Buggingham said. "But the following is what we tell ourselves behind closed company doors." She pushed a button and a new paragraph popped up.

Our mission is to locate the most polluted, vile environments on Earth and exploit those areas to make loads and loads of money no matter what the cost to public health and safety.

Buggingham and the other scientists all laughed maniacally. The scientist next to me did the exact opposite. She smacked the palm of her hand on the table and groaned, the laughter in the room drowning out her obvious displeasure.

"Sit back and relax," Buggingham said. "I am going to show a brief film to inspire everyone for the important work that lies ahead." She pulled down a large screen, the same one I used to watch documentaries on when we all went to school here.

The lights dimmed. But before everything went completely black, the scientist beside me quickly lifted her gas mask and turned to me.

"What took you so long to find a way inside?"

My mouth dropped open; my nasal cavities gasped for air.

It was Vivian.

CHAPTER 21

TECHNICAL DIFFICULTIES

How'd you get inside?" I asked.

"My mom just got a job at the catering company feeding this operation," Vivian said. "They always deliver their breakfast food the night before. I remembered that while I was waiting for my parents to crash. When I heard their snores, I snuck out, climbed into the back of a delivery truck, and hid inside a big tub of bagels. They just rolled me into the cafeteria."

"You were supposed to meet us at the Nostril tonight. We were worried about you."

Vivian shrugged. "My plan was better and

much safer than flying onto the roof of the school. Where's your bird mask?"

"I hid it on the stage," I answered.

"Remember to go back and get it. We don't want ECU to find it. Did you have any trouble getting inside?"

"Not really. A couple guards saw me on the roof. They just thought I was a turkey buzzard and moved on."

"That means the costume I designed is working. It totally disguises your identity."

An ear-piercing wail of screeching feedback filled the room. The movie screen went black and the lights turned back on.

"It appears we're having technical difficulties with the film," Buggingham said. "I've just been told the school's movie projection equipment is not working. "Fine. I love to talk so I will explain our operation and your role in making it happen."

Vivian and I sat in stunned silence as Buggingham explained ECU's true intentions for James F. Durante Elementary. The company's hyper-spectral imaging and ground-penetrating radar discovered the most noxious, smelly substance on Earth—directly under our school.

"The Gates of Smell." I whispered in Vivian's ear.

Just like there are oil pockets all over the world, there are also smell pockets—stinky underground reservoirs of ancient, coagulated dinosaur poop. Combine this with the hot, Neolithic gases of caveman bad breath, fungus feet, and armpit odor, and it's an ecological disaster waiting to happen.

That was exactly ECU's diabolical plan.

Their mission was to harness the Gates of Smell and pollute every city in the United States, starting with Denmark, New Hampshire. They, of course, would be the only company in the world with the expertise to clean up the mess and make trillions of dollars in the process. They called the goop gushing from our gym floor SPOIL— Strategic Pollution Originating Inside Layers.

Vivian and I looked at each other, the same terrified expressions on our gas-mask-clad faces. This meant this was no longer a battle for summer vacation. It was a war to save the world from ECU.

CHAPTER 22

SPOIL

Buggingham led us from the library to the Pumping Floor. Since I had seen it before, I knew what to expect. Vivian, on the other hand, was in for a complete shock.

"I can't believe that black goopy stuff is coming from the center of the earth," Vivian said, a hint of awe in her voice.

"It sure is," I replied. "And if we don't find a way to stop it, ECU is going to pollute the world."

"Gather around," Buggingham ordered. "I want to introduce you to ECU's owner, Dr. Milton Muzzle."

"Thank you, Dr. Buggingham," Muzzle said.

It was the man from the evacuation and the one who kicked me off the Pumping Floor earlier. I'd recognize his croaking voice anywhere.

"As I'm sure you learned in orientation, this seemingly innocent elementary school gymnasium is ground zero of our operation," Muzzle said and pointed toward the Gates of Smell. "Below our feet three miles into the earth's core is where numerous extinct creatures went to the bathroom. A Jurassic outhouse, if you will, creating an endless supply of SPOIL to complete our work.

"These hoses are pumping two hundred gallons of SPOIL per hour," Muzzle continued. "They are then sent to hundreds of truck tankers, waiting for my order to pollute." He glanced down at his watch. "We will be ready to launch our tankers in exactly seventy-two hours. The town of Denmark will be the first place in America to drown in SPOIL."

The more Muzzle laid out his plan, the angrier I became. It was painfully clear. He had no intention of reopening our school. We had to do something fast—me, my nose, the Not-Right Brothers, and now Vivian.

Vivian walked away from the Pumping Floor and looked out the window. After a moment, she motioned for me to join her.

"What is it?" I asked.

"There's our old gym floor," she said. "They carved it up into four giant tiles. They stacked them outside like building blocks."

"What's your point?"

"Silly. If we can get rid of ECU, we can reseal the floor. They'd fit back just like puzzle pieces."

I shook my head. "Those sections of floor probably weigh a ton. How could we ever move them?"

"That's a big problem, but I'm sure your nose can figure something out."

Buggingham clapped her hands for everyone's attention. "I have good news," she said. "Technicians have created a SPOIL-free area in the school's teachers' lounge. We now have a place we can take off our gas masks without searing our lungs to shreds. Let's assemble there in five minutes and discuss your duties further."

Muzzle, Buggingham, and the other new scientists made their way to the school library. Vivian and I didn't budge. There was no way we could take off our gas masks. They'd discover we were kids right away.

"What are we going to do?" Vivian asked.

"I think we've done enough spying for the day," I said. "Let's get out of here."

"How? I can't just slip back inside a dinner roll basket and hope they deliver me to my house. Guards and dogs are at every exit."

I lifted my gas mask and sniffed the air. SPOIL may have been dangerous for mortal noses, but my sniffer found the aroma of decaying dinosaur poop deliciously alluring. I snorted deeper and caught a familiar scent. Mixed with the overpowering odor of SPOIL was a rotting pastrami sandwich with Swiss cheese and mustard on rye.

It was Mr. Toby's lunch. He ate pastrami every day, and he had probably left it sitting on his desk the day we evacuated the school. I remembered the hatch, the one I couldn't pull open on the roof. It dropped into Mr. Toby's office. That meant it was locked from the inside. All I had to do was unlock the hatch and we'd be on the roof in seconds.

"I know the way out," I said. "Follow me."

CHAPTER 23

BY THE SKIN OF MY NOSE

Vivian and I walked around the Pumping Floor toward the gym doors. Even with the overpowering stench of SPOIL, the smell of rotting pastrami was strong. I wanted to get to the custodian's office and escape through the hatch before anyone got suspicious. But as soon as we stepped into the hallway, Buggingham stopped us.

"You two are headed the wrong way," she said. "The teachers' lounge is in the hall opposite the Pumping Floor."

"Um…we were just going to use the bathroom," I said, deepening my voice so she wouldn't know I was a kid. "The one marked *Teachers Only* near the office. We didn't want to use the one that's for children."

"There are no *children* in this building anymore and there never will be again. There is a restroom in the teachers' lounge. It's in the SPOIL-free zone so you won't have to wear masks. Follow me."

Vivian and I looked at each other. We had no choice. We had to follow Buggingham.

The teachers' lounge looked almost the same as before. There was a long table, a couch, a soda machine, and a row of shelves used for teachers' mailboxes. Against a far wall was a large, brand-new air-purifying unit. The copy machine I had hid behind on the day of the evacuation was gone. ECU had replaced it with a massive one hundred and seventy-five inch CCTV security monitor that showed several different views of the school.

Vivian stared at the screen. "They have every inch of the school covered with cameras. Look at the bottom right screen shot."

I looked down and saw what she was talking about. ECU had placed a security camera inside the custodian's office—right next to the roof hatch.

The new scientists had gathered around the table, looking at top-secret files about the operation. I nonchalantly wandered over to the table, grabbed a folder, and shoved it down the front of my pants.

"Take off your masks," Buggingham told us. "The bathroom is through that door. Hurry— we're discussing the Russian community of Nizhnevartovsk, where we first discovered SPOIL." She then joined the other scientists at the table.

Vivian and I were both desperate to breathe some fresh air, but there was no way we could take off our masks.

"What do we do now?" Vivian asked.

"Go to the bathroom," I said. "Just like Buggingham said."

When I opened the door, Vivian hesitated. "But you're a boy. We can't go to the bathroom together."

I rolled my eyes and dragged her inside. "Don't worry. I won't pee in front of you."

With the door closed and locked, we took off our gas masks. I inhaled a mighty snootful of air.

"I can't believe they actually had a mask big enough to fit over your nose," Vivian said.

"Forget my nose," I said. "We have more important things to think about. Like how to get to the hatch without ECU finding out."

"From the looks of it, there's only one thing we can do."

"Like what?"

"Bust out of this bathroom and make a run for it."

"Let's do it," I said.

Vivian and I looked at each other nervously. We took a deep breath, pulled on our gas masks, and rushed out of the teachers' lounge.

Two guards marched down the hall, dogs at their sides. We brushed by them, heading toward the custodian's office. We didn't get fifteen feet before a familiar voice called out behind us.

It was Buggingham again.

"Where do you two think you are going?" she hollered. "Orientation isn't over yet."

We ignored her and walked down the corridor as fast as we could. Buggingham shouted something to the guards. Within seconds, they were on our heels.

"Halt!" the guards ordered.

We quickened our pace to a dead sprint. I heard the snap of a chain and the sound of sharp nails scraping across the linoleum floor. The dogs were loose. A round of bullets whizzed over our heads, missing us by millimeters.

"They're shooting!" I cried out.

Mr. Toby's office was next to the kitchen at the far end of the school. We dashed past the cafeteria and dove into his office. There was the pastrami sandwich, moldy and festering with flies, sitting on his desk. A metal ladder led to the roof hatch.

"You go first," I said. "I'm right behind you."

The lock was an inside grab-handle. We gripped the long metal lever and pulled with all our might. The hatch popped open.

"Up and out," I said. "Hurry!"

Vivian slipped through the opening and onto the roof. I was just about to follow her when something grabbed the heel of my shoe. I looked down and saw a vicious-looking rottweiler ripping at my sneaker.

I tried wiggling out of my shoe, but the laces were double-knotted too tight. The guards burst into the room.

"Stop or I'll shoot!" one of the guards yelled.

My nose bumped into the drop ceiling. A cloud of dust wafted down and tickled the inside of my nostrils. My eyes felt watery; my mouth opened wide. I sneezed so hard a flood of snot blew from my honker.

The dog whimpered and released its grip on my shoe. The guards were completely soaked in mucus. One of them aimed his rifle at me and fired, but the only thing that came from the barrel was a gurgle of green boogers.

I slipped through the hatch and climbed onto the roof. Thunder boomed and lightning illuminated the night sky. The rain was showering down so hard I could barely see.

"Vivian!" I shouted. "Where are you?"

"Over here!" she hollered back. "Next to the solar panels!"

I rushed over and instructed her to climb onto my back.

She hesitated. "Are you sure you can hold my weight?"

A helmeted head popped out of the roof hatch. It was one of the guards. He had managed to free himself from my boogery quicksand.

"It's now or never!" I pleaded. "The guard is coming!"

Vivian closed her eyes and hopped onto my back. She was holding onto me so hard I could feel her sharp fingernails digging into my skin.

With a giant breath of air, I inflated my nostrils and flew us across town back to the Nostril. We had gotten away by the skin of my nose.

CHAPTER 24

NIZHNEVARTOVSK

B_y the time Vivian and I made it back to the Nostril, we looked like drowned rats. I peeled off my Super Schnoz costume and draped it over a chair to dry.

After almost getting shot and having my shoe torn apart by a rottweiler, I thought the dangerous part was over. Then I had to fly though a torrential thunderstorm. The wind was so hard it nearly blew Vivian off my back.

"You're a little late," Jimmy said when he saw Vivian.

"Late for what?" Vivian asked.

"The operation is already over," TJ said. "Schnoz

has been to the school and back again."

"Vivian was already waiting for me when I got there," I said. "She found a way in by herself."

"What are you talking about?" Mumps asked.

"Let me answer this," Vivian said, and then explained about her mom's catering company, hiding in a bucket of bagels, and disguising herself as a new scientist.

Jimmy sat up, his cheeks red with anger. "You should have told us what you were doing. ECU could have caught you and blown our whole operation."

"I agree," TJ said.

"That goes for me too," Mumps added.

"Vivian," Jimmy said. "You're fired."

Vivian's mouth dropped open. "What do you mean I'm fired?"

"Don't be silly, Jimmy," I said. "We need her. She's been inside the building and knows the layout."

"We can't trust her. You heard it yourself. She's sneaking around, doing her own thing. We have to be a team. For all we know, she's a spy for ECU."

"I'm not a spy!" Vivian fired back. "I'm a part of the team. We need each other."

"ECU's guards almost killed us," I said. "Trust me. She isn't working with them."

I spent the next twenty minutes filling them in on what had happened inside the school. As far as I was concerned, Vivian was already part of our team. Jimmy, TJ, and Mumps huddled in the corner, talking among each other, deciding what to do. We were a democracy, and I was only one vote.

"Okay," Jimmy said finally. "Schnoz, if you trust her then we will too. But she can't just go wandering off by herself. I won't be responsible for the safety of a defenseless girl."

Vivian held up her fists. "I could beat you up easy. Stick 'em up!"

"Stop it!" I hollered. "We can't fight ourselves and ECU at the same time. Vivian and I have a lot more to tell you about what we discovered inside their operation. We only have sixty-seven hours to save our town. Let's get to work."

The morning sun had just peeked over the White Mountains when Vivian and I finished our briefing on ECU's hideous plan, everything from SPOIL and the Gates of Smell to their planned environmental attack on the town of Denmark.

"We have to defeat them," Jimmy said. "I cannot—will not be sitting in Mrs. Field's classroom come July."

"I second that," TJ added.

"I third it," Mumps chimed.

"Then what's the plan?" Vivian asked.

All eyes turned to me, I was the one with the superpowers.

"The answer is simple," I said. "We destroy ECU and seal the Gates of Smell forever."

"And how are we supposed to do that?" Mumps asked.

The Top-Secret Report.

I'd swiped it from the teachers' lounge inside the school. It was still down the front of my pants. During the wet flight back to the Nostril, I'd forgotten all about it. I tugged it out of my underwear and laid it on the table. The folder was actually a book, bound in leather, with the words *ECU—Commission on Takeover, Destruction, and Profit* stamped across the front.

"Maybe this can help us," I said. "It's a top-secret document I swiped from ECU."

We spent the next hour poring over the pages. The book was broken up into three sections. The first part was all technical—how to discover sources of SPOIL, and then the science of extracting it from the ground. The second part was just plain horrifying. It explained in gruesome detail about ECU's first SPOIL operation in Northern Russia in a town called Nizhnevartovsk. I remembered

Buggingham mentioning that name in the teachers' lounge before our escape.

ECU's scientists had located a pocket of SPOIL underneath the city's community center. Just like in our town, they unleashed a toxic smell. After convincing government officials they could clean it up, they took over the building and started pumping out barrels of SPOIL. When they had enough of the goopy, smelly liquid, they systematically saturated the town. The toxic substance destroyed entire neighborhoods, people lost their homes, and some lost their lives. ECU then swooped in like heroes, claiming they could clean everything up—for a hefty price. They had made twenty-seven million dollars on one little Russian town.

"They could make twice as much in New Hampshire," Vivian said. "America's the richest country in the world."

"Probably five times," Mumps added.

"Turn to part three," Jimmy said. "Let see what it has to say."

Part three was titled *Denmark, New Hampshire*.

My stomach churned like I had just swallowed a hunk of moldy bologna. From the frightened looks on my friends' faces, they felt the same way. Denmark was going to suffer the same fate as Nizhnevartovsk if we didn't stop them.

Just as Jimmy opened his mouth to comment, his mother hollered from the kitchen window.

"Jimmy! Tell your friends it's time to go home. Sleepover is officially over."

"Great," Jimmy said. "Now what do we do?"

"Let's go home, get some rest, and make an appearance for our parents," I said. "We'll meet back at the Nostril at noon."

I opened the door to leave, and that's when I realized I had forgotten my Mardi Gras mask back on the school stage.

CHAPTER 25

THE CAYENNE CANNON

I didn't get back to the Nostril until almost twelve thirty. Vivian and the Not-Right Brothers were waiting for me. They weren't very happy.

"You're late, Schnoz," Jimmy said.

"Sorry," I said. "My mom made me cut the lawn. I had to wait for the grass to dry out from last night's storm."

Jimmy pointed to the clock on TJ's laptop. You're the one who said we only had sixty-seven hours to save our town."

"Stop bickering," Vivian said. "We have to concentrate on our game plan."

"But we don't have a plan," Mumps said.

I retrieved my Super Schnoz costume from the back of a chair.

"By the way, I forgot the Mardi Gras mask when we left the school last night," I said. "Do you have another one?"

"A mask is vital to keeping your identity a secret," Vivian huffed. "Your nose is as recognizable in this town as the Old Man of the Mountain. Lucky for you my parents have a bunch of masks."

Vivian charged across the street to her house and brought back another mask. This one had all yellow feathers and a big yellow beak. Little black beads outlined the eyes.

"I'm not wearing this," I said. "I'll look like Big Bird."

"Tough," Jimmy said. "You should have thought about that when you lost the other one."

"Take a deep breath, guys," Vivian said. "I don't care what the mask looks like as long as it disguises Schnoz's nose. Let's break down the operation, starting from the beginning. What should happen first?"

"Sneak into the school without alerting the security guards," said TJ.

"Schnoz, you secretly fly us all on the roof and we'll slip down the hatch," Vivian said.

"Sounds good in theory, Viv," I said. "But I can't just fly people one at time. It's too dangerous, more chances of them spotting us."

"Then fly us all at once," Jimmy said. "That way you only do one trip. I can make a harness with my sister's sewing machine, one big enough to hold all four of us. Can you still get airborne will all the extra weight?"

I nodded my nose. "As long as I have enough wind in my nostrils it shouldn't be a problem."

"Good," TJ said. "Issue solved. What's next?"

"We have to deal with all the security guards, vicious dogs, armored tanks, and attack helicopters," Mumps said.

The Nostril grew quiet. Sneaking into the school was easy, but battling dozens of armed guards with high-tech military equipment was another matter altogether.

"What about pepper?" Jimmy said quietly.

"What are you talking about?" I asked.

"Remember when I wanted to get out of a pop quiz in Mrs. Field's class? You snorted a few grains of pepper and sneezed so hard the fire alarm went off."

"The walls of the school actually shook," Mumps added.

"So, that's your grand plan," I said sarcastically. "You want me to snort some pepper, set off the fire alarms, and hope it scares away the bad guys. That's a ridiculous idea."

"I think it's a fabulous idea!" Vivian exclaimed. "But instead of using plain black pepper, Schnoz uses cayenne pepper."

"What's cayenne pepper?" Jimmy asked.

"It's super hot, a hundred times more powerful than black pepper. My dad loves spicy food. He uses the stuff to make five-alarm Buffalo wings. If just a little bit of wimpy black pepper can make the walls of the school shake, just imagine what a whole jar of cayenne can do."

I paced around the room, index finger tapping my chin, thinking. Vivian was onto something. The sneeze that set off the fire alarm was powerful, kind of like a firecracker going off inside my nose. If the cayenne pepper was a lot stronger it could be like a…

"A cayenne cannon!" Vivian shouted, as if reading my mind. "Those tanks, guards, and helicopters won't stand a chance!"

Everyone cheered. We were all excited to invade the school and blow ECU to kingdom come. Twenty minutes later, after a quick stop at Vivian's house to raid her cupboards of cayenne, we were standing in the middle of the Denmark Auto Salvage Yard. There were piles of junked cars and trucks as far as the eye could see.

Vivian pulled out a huge jar of cayenne pepper. "Let's have a test," she said. "Snort some of this, point your nose at one of those wrecked eighteen-wheelers, and see what happens."

Everyone stood back for safety. I held the jar in front of my nose and huffed with all my breath. The sting of the pepper hit me instantly. It felt like a million tiny razor blades were shooting up my nasal cavity.

Then it happened.

A sneeze blasted out of my nose so hard it split the truck in half and sent the pieces flying across the salvage yard.

Vivian grabbed the jar of cayenne from my hand and gave me a huge hug.

"You did it, Schnoz! You're going to save our town!"

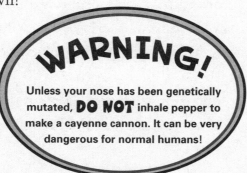

WARNING!

Unless your nose has been genetically mutated, **DO NOT** inhale pepper to make a cayenne cannon. It can be very dangerous for normal humans!

CHAPTER 26

THE BATTLE BEGINS

The harness Jimmy sewed together worked great. He even decorated it with a bunch of feathers to make it blend with the turkey buzzard appearance. The lift was rough at first because of the extra weight. TJ, Mumps, and Vivian were fine, but Jimmy's chunky behind weighed a ton! After a couple false starts, I managed to get enough wind in my nostrils and soar into the clouds.

The sky was dusky, teetering on the edge of day and night. Two guards now patrolled the roof—probably because of my escape with Vivian the night before. Fortunately, they were on the far side of the school nowhere near the hatch. The guards easily saw me floating in the air, but they didn't give me a second glance. They must have thought we were nothing but a fat turkey buzzard.

Vivian and the Not-Right Brothers cautiously crawled from the harness. I unhooked the straps around my back. We were ready for action.

"You're going to need these," Vivian said, handing me six large jars of cayenne pepper.

I stuffed the weapons into my utility belt and led everyone to the roof hatch. "I hope the guards forgot to lock this last night," I said and then tugged the handle. It popped right open.

Vivian and the Not-Right Brothers disappeared down the hatch.

We had everything planned out. My job was mostly on the outside, disposing of the heavy armor positioned around the school grounds. Vivian and the Not-Right Brothers' work was on the inside, figuring out how to sabotage the Pumping Floor operation and stop the flow of SPOIL.

I crept along the edge of the school, assessing the scene. Dozens of armed guards with dogs ringed the perimeter. The attack helicopter sat on its pad like a giant dragonfly. Ten M172 armored flamethrower tanks were poised ready and willing. Another dozen or so Stryker ground combat vehicles rounded out the enemy defenses.

Fighting them would be extremely dangerous. I prayed I had enough cayenne ammo to finish the job.

Just as I was about to fly off the roof, a bullet whizzed past my ear.

"Darn it!" yelled a guard on the ground below me. "Missed that bird by a feather!"

Another guard yanked out his weapon. "Watch this, Ernie. I'm an expert turkey buzzard hunter. I'll bring that mangy thing down in one shot."

He aimed and fired. The shot missed, but just barely. It nearly took off my beak.

The battle had begun.

I grabbed a cayenne jar from my belt, sniffed, and sneezed right at them. The force knocked the guns out of their hands and blew them across the road into the baseball field.

The commotion alerted the flame-throwing tanks. I flew to the ground, took a quick snort of pepper, and knocked out eight of them right away. The last two were on me fast, red-hot flames puffing from their barrels.

Before I could react to the tanks, the Stryker combat vehicles were on the move. In a matter of seconds, they had me surrounded. I breathed

in some more pepper and took out half the Strykers and another tank. Their metal armor exploded into a thousand scraps, scattering all over the playground.

The last flame-throwing tank raced in my direction. As I sneezed, the tank fired. My cayenne blast and the tank's scorching flames collided together. The explosion of heat was so blistering it melted the tank and the rest of the Strykers like crayons inside a microwave.

My nose hairs were singed, and my cape was on fire. I hit the ground, rolling around to put out the flames. Ground troops raced in my direction. I grabbed a jar of cayenne and started to sniff. That's when a voice rang out over a loudspeaker.

"Super Schnoz, stand down your nose!"

It was Muzzle. I recognized his voice instantly.

"How do you know my name?" I cried, taking a big whiff of more pepper.

"I know because your friends told me. They are now my captives. Stand down or you will never see them alive again!"

I stopped sniffing. My heart raced with panic.

"What are you talking about?"

"We have captured your accomplices. Listen to this."

Jimmy's small, terrified voice came over the loudspeaker. "It's true, Schnoz. They captured us all. Muzzle said if you don't surrender, he's going to throw us into the Gates of Smell."

Every olfactory receptor in my nasal cavity urged me to fight on. I wanted to sneeze ECU's army back to the Stone Age, but I couldn't risk my friends' lives. If Muzzle was evil enough to pollute every city in America, he would have no problem throwing kids into a pit of dinosaur poop.

I dropped my cayenne, raised my nose in the air, and surrendered.

CHAPTER 27

INTERROGATION

A gang of armed guards tied my hands behind my back and led me into the school. They marched me past the main office and into the school library. I saw Jimmy, Mumps, and TJ tied to chairs, but I didn't see Vivian anywhere. My friends weren't wearing gas masks, so ECU must have made the library a SPOIL-free zone just like the teachers' lounge.

One of the guards shoved me into a seat beside Jimmy. He held up a pair of scissors. "One sniff out of you, Super Schnoz, and I'll snip off that snout quicker than you can say nose hair. Got it?"

I nodded. The guard stuffed the scissors into his belt and walked away.

When he was out of earshot, I whispered to Jimmy, "Where's Vivian? Are they interrogating her?"

"They didn't catch her," Jimmy said. "They think we're the only ones. As far as I know, she's still roaming the school trying to figure out a way to sabotage the flow of SPOIL."

I let out a huge sigh of relief. At least they didn't get us all.

The door opened and in walked a man and woman. I overheard a guard address them as Dr. Buggingham and Dr. Muzzle. I could finally see their putrid faces. Buggingham was tall and young. Her skin was as white as a snowball and her eyes were like two sky-blue marbles. Muzzle looked the exact opposite. He was old and wrinkly, with a fake, dark tan and unnaturally white teeth that could probably glow in the dark.

"Well, it appears we have found your weakness, Super Schnoz," Muzzle said, an evil grin plastered across his face. "Friendship."

"What are you going to do with us?" I barked at him.

"You'll know in due time. But first we need to pump some information from you boys."

"Who else knows about our operation in the school?" Buggingham interjected.

"Nobody," Jimmy said. "It's just us."

Buggingham gritted her teeth and tweaked Jimmy's earlobes. "I wasn't talking to you! I was asking Super Schnoz."

"The whole world knows about it," I said. "Homeland Security will be here any moment so you better let us go."

Muzzle threw back his head and laughed. "My dear Super Schnoz, you not only have an exceptionally large nose, but also an exceptionally large imagination. To the outside world, ECU is a heroic savior of the environment. A few months ago I received a medal as a Hero of the Russian Federation from their president. We saved the town of Nizhnevartovsk from an environmental disaster."

"You didn't save anybody from anything! I know what you did. You polluted the town on purpose. Most of those people lost everything, and some lost their lives!"

"And you will lose your life too," Buggingham said. "Right after we get some information."

Muzzle pulled a bird mask with a large beak from a paper bag. I recognized it instantly. It was the one I had forgotten on the stage.

"One of my guards found this," Muzzle said, stroking the feathers. "At first, I didn't know what to make of it. We had emptied the school of nearly everything, so I figured our men had overlooked it. But now I know perfectly well this mask is yours, isn't it, Super Schnoz? It was you and one of your friends who posed as scientists and then escaped through the roof hatch. How did you breach our security? It's the most sophisticated in the world."

"I'm not telling you anything!" I spit at him.

Muzzle yanked off the mask I was wearing. He gently rubbed the bridge of my nose. "Fascinating," he said. "You're just a dim-witted juvenile like the rest, probably a student here. I think we are going to keep you alive for a while, my nosy friend. We may have some use for this lethal appendage of yours."

Just then the library door flew open. A scientist wearing a gas mask and white lab coat burst into the room.

"Dr. Buggingham, Dr. Muzzle," the scientist said, "we need you on the Pumping Floor. There's an emergency."

"Come with us, guards. These insurgents aren't going anywhere," Buggingham said as she, Muzzle, and our guards slipped on gas masks and rushed out the door.

The scientist didn't budge.

She just stood at the doorway, staring at us, and then took off her gas mask.

"Vivian!" I cried out. "I thought I'd never see you again!"

CHAPTER 28

FREE SODA

Quick!" I ordered. "Untie us before they come back!"

Vivian rushed over and loosened our bonds.

"They knotted those ropes so tight it was cutting off my circulation," Mumps said, massaging his hands.

"Me too," TJ added. "I thought my arms were going to fall off."

I peered out the library door. The hallway was clear, but I knew it wouldn't be for long.

"Throw on these gas masks," I said. "We have to get moving before they come back."

"Aren't you going to wear one too?" Jimmy asked me.

I picked my Mardi Gras mask off the floor and pulled it over my nose. "This is the only mask I need. Besides, I want to smell their fear when we come to destroy them."

Vivian handed me the last jar of cayenne and led us down the hallway. Two guards tried to stop us near the nurse's office, but I quickly put them away with a peppery sneeze.

A sharp pain sliced inside my right nostril. I reached up, rubbed my nose, and felt something warm and wet.

Blood.

"You have a nosebleed," Vivian said, a look of concern washing across her face. I knew right away it was from the cayenne pepper. The stuff must have been eating away the lining of my nasal passages.

"I'm fine," I said. "We have to keep moving."

Down the hall, outside the Pumping Floor, I heard Buggingham's voice. "There's nothing wrong here," she said. "Hurry, let's get back to the interrogation."

"Follow me," Vivian whispered. "I found what we need to put those poop slurpers out of commission forever."

We dashed through the cafeteria, heading to the teachers' lounge. The room was exactly as

I remembered it, from the air-purification unit to the one-hundred-and-seventy-five-inch CCTV security monitor. Next to the air-purification unit was a vending machine stuffed with soda.

"Grab as many cans of soda as you can carry," Vivian instructed. "We're going to dump them into the computers that control the flow of SPOIL. Sugar water and motherboards don't mix."

"But the sign says it costs a dollar a can," Jimmy said. "We don't have any money."

"Teachers don't have to pay for soda," Vivian said. "It's written in their teaching contract."

"Then I want to be a teacher when I grow up!" Mumps gushed.

We pushed the vending machine buttons. Out flew can after free can of soda—orange-flavored, grape, lemon, lime, cherry, cream, root beer.

"They set up the computers in the gym equipment storage room," Vivian said. "That's right next to the Pumping Floor. The door is heavily guarded and locked at all times."

"How do we get inside?" Jimmy asked.

"Leave that up to me," I said. "You guys wait

here. When you hear me sneeze and things start exploding, that's your cue to rush into the computer room and drown those babies."

"There's only one jar of cayenne pepper left," Vivian said. "What if you run out?"

I stepped over to the window and looked out. It was dark, but I knew from memory what was there—the kickball diamond, the playground, soccer field, basketball court, parking lot—places that were now infected with ECU's greedy disease.

"I won't run out," I said. "And even if I do, my nose will shrivel up and rot before I allow Muzzle and his minions to pollute our town."

I raced out of the room straight into the stinky rump of the beast.

CHAPTER 29
THE DOWNWARD SPIRAL

The stinky rump of the beast was a crater-sized hole in the center of our gym floor.

I tilted back the jar of cayenne pepper, inhaled deeply, and nearly passed out on the floor. The pain was excruciating. It felt like my nose was on fire. Drops of blood soaked the front of my Super Schnoz costume, but I had to keep moving.

It didn't take long for me to find trouble.

Buggingham and Muzzle had discovered our escape and sent out an alert. I was a marked nose. Every ECU employee on school grounds was on the lookout for me and my friends. Four rifle-toting guards confronted me in front of my old classroom.

"Ah…choo!" I fired, sending out a lethal, bloody snotball that knocked the guards off their feet.

More of the enemy raced in my direction. I sneezed my way closer to the Pumping Floor; each pepper-spiced booger bomb was like a razor blade ripping the inside of my nose. Guards collapsed to the left and right of me, others went sailing through the gym doors and into the parking lot. I checked my ammo—only two tablespoons left. I was saving those for Buggingham and Muzzle.

By the time I made it to the Pumping Floor, the rest of Muzzle's men had abandoned the operation. At the mere sight of my nose, they dropped their weapons and high-tailed it off school grounds.

The only thing left to do was to figure out a way to get the gym floor back in place and seal the Gates of Smell.

But Muzzle had other plans.

A girl's frightened voice screamed out from behind me. I turned and saw the aging polluter with Vivian in his grasp. I reached for the last of my cayenne pepper. Muzzle rushed toward the Gates of Smell, tugging Vivian along with him. When he got to the edge of the pit, he dangled her over the side.

"One sniff closer, Super Schnoz, and the girl dives into the stinky abyss!" Muzzle screamed at me.

I stopped dead in my tracks. He had me. There was no way I would ever risk Vivian's life—even if it meant going to school all summer.

"You're a fool, my nosy friend!" Muzzle

cackled. "Did you really think you could stop me? Now, I want you to raise your nose in the air and back slowly away from the Pumping Floor."

I hesitated, not knowing what to do.

"Do it!" Muzzle hollered. "Or the girl goes into the pit!"

The sound of a helicopter's rotating wings blasted my ears. The noise was so loud I could barely make out Muzzle's words. I turned and saw an attack helicopter piloted by Buggingham hovering outside the gym doors. A rope ladder lowered to the ground.

"Back away," Muzzle warned.

I did as he ordered, moving slowly toward the far end of the gym.

"Hurry, Milton!" I heard Buggingham shout through the whine of the helicopter.

A computer voice rang out from an intercom system, "Building will detonate in three minutes and fifty-five seconds."

"What was that?" I shouted.

Muzzle cackled and dangled Vivian farther over the pit. "Did you really think you could defeat me, Super Schnoz? We have programmed the computers to self-detonate in exactly four minutes. This whole school will blow to smithereens. SPOIL will spew everywhere and flood the streets of Denmark. And guess what? My company will be back to clean it up just like in Russia!"

Muzzle flung Vivian with all his might, sending her on a downward spiral into the Gates of Smell.

CHAPTER 30

FREEFALL

Muzzle ran to the dangling rope ladder, grabbed hold, and lifted off with his accomplice into the night sky. I raced to the pit, plunging nose first into the Gates of Smell.

My stomach heaved into my throat. My cape whipped around my face, temporarily blinding me. When I could finally see, I glimpsed Vivian just ahead, free-falling toward the nastiest, smelliest, gooiest, most foul substance the world has ever known.

With a flight trick I learned from watching a documentary about red-tailed hawks, I pinned my arms to my sides, positioned my body at an angle, and dove at breakneck speed. I didn't know

146

how far the Gates of Smell spiraled into the earth's core, but I knew my friend was a goner if she fell directly into a pocket of greasy SPOIL.

"Help me, Schnoz!" I heard Vivian scream in the darkness.

I was close, very close. A flame shot out from the side of the pit, illuminating the gloom. There she was, a few feet from me. I reached out. Our fingers touched. I clamped down harder, grabbed her elbow, and pulled her into my chest. She clung to me like a frightened baby chimp.

"We're going to die," Vivian whimpered.

I knew from reading ECU's Top-Secret Report that SPOIL had the consistency of quicksand. If Vivian and I landed in it, we'd drown for sure. I tried inflating my nostrils to float us to the surface, but the pain was too much. Every time I took a deep breath, the scabs forming inside my nose burst open. Blood and mucus dripped from my nose like a leaky faucet. My super schnoz was useless.

The bottom of the hole lay below us just a few hundred feet away. The Gates of Smell was more hideous than I had ever imagined. Bubbling, crackling, oozing, ancient poop, the smell was almost too much even for my well-seasoned honker.

The cayenne. Another sniff would probably kill me, but I had no choice. It was our only chance.

I managed to twist off the lid and inhale the last two tablespoons of pepper. A stab of skull-splitting pain sliced through my nasal cavity.

"Owww!" I cried out. The sting was so intense it felt like someone had just smacked me in the face with a concrete block.

I sneezed with all my might. Snot mixed with blood and boogers blasted from my wounded nose. The mucus splashed into the pit of SPOIL. The goop fizzed and smoked, gurgling like a fire-breathing dragon ready to swallow us whole.

"What's happening?" Vivian asked.

"It's some weird chemical reaction between my snot and SPOIL!" I said. "Brace for impact!"

Just as we were about to plunge into SPOIL, a huge air bubble the size of a swimming pool formed on its surface. We collided against the bubble and it popped, releasing a rush of

disgusting, stinky, poopy air. The rush of foul wind inflated my nostrils like two balloons. The pain made me cry out in agony, but I didn't care. Vivian and I were drifting upward on a breeze of old dinosaur poop!

We blasted from the pit so high we nearly hit the gym roof. Everything was soaked with SPOIL, but we didn't care. We were smelly but safe. It was such a thrill to be on solid ground, I nearly forgot about Muzzle's plan to blow up the school and flood SPOIL into our town.

Fortunately, Jimmy, Mumps, and TJ were right on task.

As Vivian and I sat there soaked in slimy SPOIL, the Not-Right Brothers went to work. They peeled open can after can of sugary soda and poured the contents over ECU's main computer. The computer voice from the intercom counted down the moment of detonation.

Twenty…nineteen…eighteen…seventeen…sixteen…

"Hurry, you guys!" I pleaded. "We're running out of time!"

"We're going as fast as we can!" Jimmy yelled back.

The remaining seconds flew past like the flick of a booger. The boys had soaked the entire computer system. So much that they were standing ankle-high in a puddle of pop.

Five…four…three…two…one…

I lowered my head, shielded Vivian with my cape, and awaited the explosion.

The only thing that blew up was the computer system.

"We did it," Vivian said, exhausted from her ordeal. "We saved the town."

Jimmy cracked open a can of soda and took a huge swig. "And we saved summer vacation," he added.

CHAPTER 31

SUMMER VACATION

An announcement came over the PA system as we sat in Mrs. Field's room, cleaning out our desks. It was Principal Cyrano, wishing us a fun and safe summer vacation.

"This has certainly been a challenging year for all of us," The principal said. "After all the problems we had in school with the odor and our first environmental cleaning company quitting and leaving us with a huge mess, we should all be very proud of our patience. And we only had to be in school until June twenty-fourth!"

The kids in Mrs. Field's class cheered and pumped their fists in the air.

"ECU didn't quit," Jimmy said to me. "We kicked them out."

"It stinks that only the five of us know the truth," Mumps said.

"We're heroes," TJ added. "Our faces should be plastered all over the news. The principal should pin us with medals. Marvel should make a comic book about us—Super Schnoz and the Not-Right Brothers!"

"Don't forget me," Vivian said, clipping a purple hair extension to her ponytail. "I'm the brains of this operation."

"Sorry," TJ said. "Super Schnoz, the Not-Right Brothers, and Vivian."

Some recognition sounded good to me. Kids had been teasing me about my honker since nursery school. It was about time they saw the real me. I was no longer just a kid with a big nose ripe for mockery. I had a mission—to fight evil and boldly smell where no kid has smelled before!

"I vote we tell everybody," Jimmy said. "Schnoz, put on your costume and fly over the school. After that, rip up the gym floor and show everyone the Gates of Smell. Then the world will know the real story about ECU."

Vivian snatched my backpack away before I could grab the cape and Mardi Gras mask. "You guys can't be serious," she said. "I thought you were just joking around."

"It's no joke," Mumps said. "We deserve some credit."

"And a medal from Principal Cyrano," TJ chimed in.

"If you breathe one word of Super Schnoz's true identity or what happened inside this school, not only are our lives in danger but also the lives of our friends and family."

"Don't be a drama queen," Jimmy said.

"Was I being a drama queen when Muzzle threw me into the Gates of Smell? I'd be dead right now if it wasn't for Schnoz."

We all grew silent. The lure of fame and fortune was strong, but deep down I knew we had to keep everything a secret.

"Vivian's right," I said. "Muzzle and

Buggingham are still on the loose. They've seen our faces. If we start blabbing, they'll know our names too."

"And they'll know exactly where to find us," Vivian added. "ECU will be out for revenge."

The Not-Right Brothers reluctantly gave in and we vowed to keep my identity and our operation top secret.

When the end-of-school buzzer rang, I cleaned out my locker and said my good-byes. Vivian was off to guitar camp, TJ to Camp Noogiewagga, Mumps to Cape Cod, and Jimmy to Mt. Washington with his dad.

I hopped on my bike and pedaled toward the outskirts of town. My smell tour was already behind and I wanted to get sniffing. My first stop was the town dump. It was a potpourri of scents. But when I got there, nothing seemed to excite me. Rotting garbage, smoldering car tires, and decaying rat carcasses held little fascination after inhaling the odors locked inside the Gates of Smell.

In the distance, I heard the familiar whine of

helicopter wings. It may have been Muzzle and Buggingham coming back for more or it may have been the local TV news helicopter.

I reached inside my backpack, threw on my Super Schnoz cape and Mardi Gras mask, and took a big whiff of cayenne pepper.

With one nostril open for trouble, I wasn't about to take any chances.

NOW IN PAPERBACK!

Super Schnoz and the Invasion of the Snore Snatchers • 978-0-8075-7561-1 • $6.99

TURN THE PAGE FOR A
SNEAK PEEK OF

AND THE
SECRET
OF STRANGE

Super Schnoz and the Secret of Strange • 978-0-8075-7562-8 • $14.99

CHAPTER 1

STRANGE SCENT

Schnoz, what's that weird smell?" Jimmy asked me one day while TJ, Mumps, Vivian, and I were cruising on our bikes down Main Street.

I flared my nostrils and inhaled the luscious, intoxicating scent. My nose hairs tingled with joy. My olfactory bulbs throbbed with delight. The wonderful smell had been wafting in the crisp autumn air of Denmark, New Hampshire, for weeks and my nose could barely contain its excitement.

"That smell isn't weird," I answered. "It's *Strange*, as in Jean Paul Puanteur's *Strange*."

"Huh?" TJ grunted.

"*Strange* is the name of an extremely popular

unisex perfume." Vivian said, steering her bike toward Dr. Wackjöb's Gecko Glue® and Snore Cure Mist® factory. "Every teenager and adult in town wears it."

"What's unisex mean?" Jimmy asked.

I hit the brakes and my bike skidded to a stop. "It means the perfume is suitable for both sexes, male and female.

TJ laughed. "Perfume's for girls."

"Don't tell that to my dad," Mumps said. "He's been spraying himself with Strange every morning for a month."

"My mom loves it, too," Vivian added. "She's goes through a bottle every two weeks."

"Jean Paul Puanteur is the greatest perfumer in the world!" I proclaimed. "He's the Mozart of odor, the Picasso of aroma!"

"Schnoz, let me give you a piece of advice," Jimmy razzed. "Don't let the other guys in school know you like perfume. It could be seriously bad for your honker health."

Before I could respond, one of Dr. Wackjöb's delivery trucks whizzed past us. His Gecko Glue®

and Snore Cure Mist® products were selling like hotcakes around the world. In fact, they were so successful that Filthy Rich Review magazine had featured the company on the cover of its October issue. But the best thing about the business was that it employed hundreds of local people. My mom even got a job there as a quality control supervisor.

"I don't care what anyone thinks," I said to Jimmy after the truck had turned the corner. "I'm not just a one-sniff pony who only likes the smells of dog poop, armpits, and rotting road kill. I'm a connoisseur of the sweeter scents in life too, you know."

"The art of mixing herb oil, spices, and tree resins to make different fragrances goes all the way back to ancient Babylon," Vivian said. "Perfuming is as old as civilization itself."

TJ rolled his eyes. "Ancient or not, I still say perfume is for girls."

"Stop being a sexist!" Vivian yelled and then held up her fists. "Do you want a bop on the chin?"

"I'm not six!" TJ fired back. "I turned eleven two months ago."

"I said you were a *sexist*, dork butt. A person who stereotypes people based on their gender."

"She's right, TJ," I said. "Apologize. Vivian's smarter and tougher than all of you Not-Right Brothers put together."

TJ kicked a rock. "I'm sorry, but I didn't mean anything by it. I just assumed only girls wore perfume, that's all."

"Well, now you know different," Vivian said. "Let's hurry up and get to Dr. Wackjöb's office. I'm starving."

Every Wednesday was early release day from school so the teachers could have meetings. We got out at noon and, weather permitting, always rode our bikes to Dr. Wackjöb's office for lunch. As we rode down the street toward the factory, I inhaled the overpowering smell of *Strange* that drifted through the Denmark air.

Distinguishing between the perfume's different ingredients proved difficult at first, but soon my powerful olfactory receptors downloaded the parts directly into my mental scent dictionary. The perfume's base was ethyl alcohol and distilled water. Next, I sniffed a tantalizing blend of essential oils like lavender, jasmine, sandalwood, and bergamot. I could tell the perfume was of the highest quality because all the ingredients were natural, not one synthetic fragrance in the mix.

The security guard at Dr. Wackjöb's opened the factory gates and we rolled into the parking lot. I leaned my bike on the rack, took one stop toward the office door, and that's when I sensed another extremely subtle, barely detectable ingredient in the *Strange* concoction. The odor stopped me in my tracks. My nose lifted into the air, huffing like a crazed bloodhound at the scent particles floating on the wind.

"What's wrong, Schnoz?" Vivian asked. "You look like you just smelled a ghost."

"I smell something, all right," I said, my heart thumping. "And I have no idea what it is."

"But you know practically every smell on earth," Mumps said.

I scanned my mental scent dictionary front to back, starting with the pungent odor of a crushed ant to the cheesy aroma of baked ziti. There was nothing, not one tiny whiff of the *Strange* scent.

CHAPTER 2

FRENCH JASMINE

Dr. Wackjöb was chatting on the phone when his secretary escorted us into his office. The overwhelming stench of fresh Hákarl blasted up my nostrils. I loved the smell of fermented, urine-soaked shark meat, but the Icelandic delicacy made Vivian and the Not-Right Brothers nearly gag.

Jimmy pulled his t-shirt up over his nose. "Why does Dr. Wackjöb have to eat that disgusting Hákarl every single day for lunch?"

"I don't like the smell, either," Vivian said. "But we have to give the guy a break. The doctor was a laughing stock in his native Iceland and had to flee. Hákarl reminds him of home."

"Hákarl reminds me of an unflushed toilet," Mumps said with a grimace.

"So nice to hear from you, Pierre, and I hope to speak with you soon." Dr. Wackjöb said and then hung up the phone. He pointed to three large pizza boxes sitting on a conference table. "One is plain, one is pepperoni, and the other is black olives and mushrooms. Please, help yourselves."

Vivian, the Not-Brothers, and I tore into the pizzas like starving rescue dogs. Dr. Wackjöb tied a bib around his neck and popped slices of Hákarl into his mouth. He chewed very slowly, savoring each and every shark pee–flavored bite.

While the gang munched away, my nose drifted off to the mysterious smell locked inside *Strange*. The fragrance resembled vanilla, but the unknown aroma was way more earthy, funky, and bold than any variety I had ever come across during my scent gathering expeditions. Only a master like Jean Paul Puanteur could confuse my world-class sniffer like this!

Most kids my age have posters of actors,

musicians, and athletes hanging on their bedroom walls. As for me, I have only a small, 8x10-framed picture of Jean Paul Puanteur. I had clipped the photo from a *National Geographic* magazine article about the art and science of making perfume. He is standing in a field of extremely rare and expensive French jasmine, a brilliant orange sun high in the sky. The man is a scent artist of the highest order.

A set of greasy fingers snapped in front of my face.

"Earth to Schnoz," Vivian said, ripping me out of my French jasmine daze. "You're staring blankly into space. What are you thinking about?"

"*Strange*," I said.

TJ fanned the air in front of his face. "I wish I had a bottle of *Strange* right now. I'd spray it around the room to get rid of the Hákarl stink!"

Dr. Wackjob laughed. "Iceland's secret shark recipe goes all the way back to the time of Vikings. What is this *Strange* you speak of?"

"*Strange* is a ridiculously popular perfume," Mumps answered. "Everybody's wearing the stuff."

"I'm a huge fan of the perfuming arts," I said.

"But there's one ingredient in *Strange* that my snuffer can't sniff out."

Dr. Wackjöb raised his white, bushy eyebrows. "You, the one and only Super Schnoz, cannot recognize a scent? I don't believe it. Your nose is to smells like Einstein's brain is to physics."

"Well, this is one odor equation I have yet to crack."

"I don't know anything about the perfume business," Dr. Wackjöb continued. "But just like my company has a secret ingredient—synthetic setae developed from the sticky pads on a gecko's feet—I would assume perfumers use secret ingredients as well."

I shrugged. "You're probably right, but if I don't figure out that smell and add it to my scent dictionary I'm going to blow a booger!"

"Perhaps I should call back Pierre and ask him."

"Who's Pierre?" Vivian asked.

"He's the gentleman I was talking to on the phone as you arrived for lunch. He's a Frenchman, an old friend of mine from when I studied geology for a year at the *University*

Lille Nord de France. I hadn't spoken with him in thirty years. He phoned me out of blue after reading about my successful business in *Filthy Rich Review* magazine."

"Why would this Pierre person know about secret ingredients found in perfume?" I asked.

"Gríðarstór Nef, my old friend's full name is Pierre du Voleur, owner of the Français Scent Company, makers of fine perfumes and fragrances."

I sat up in my seat, nose hairs quivering with excitement. "Can you ask him about the mystery ingredient in *Strange*?"

"That won't do any good," Vivian said.

"Why?"

"*Strange* is made by Jean Paul Puanteur, a completely different company. Coke would never give up its secret soda formula to Pepsi. Why would two rival perfume companies share ingredients?"

"She's right, Schnoz," Jimmy said. "If you want to figure out that smell, you'll have to huff it out for yourself."

The scent receptors inside my honker deflated

a little. Now I knew how Peter Parker felt when he had to battle Venom in the *Amazing Spider Man #6*. The task would be daunting, but I had never met a smell my nose couldn't defeat, and *Strange* was not going to be the first.